GESUALDO BUFALINO was born at Comiso, Sicily, in 1920. He studied literature at Catania and Palermo, and was a teacher by profession, turning author only after his retirement in 1976. He started his first novel, *The Plague-spreader's Tale*, in 1950, but it was only in 1981, after he took the discarded manuscript out of the drawer and reworked it, that it was published; it won the Premio Campiello. This has been followed by a succession of remarkable novels and other works, including *Blind Argus* ("a construct of time and memory, artful, and full of delight" *Scotsman*) and *Night's Lies*, which won the author Italy's top literary award, the Premio Strega.

PATRICK CREAGH won the John Florio Prize for his translation of *Blind Argus*. In addition to his translation of *Night's Lies* he has brought to an English-language readership the work of many leading Italian writers, including Vitaliano Brancati, Sebastiano Vassalli, Claudio Magris, Marta Morazzoni and Salvatore Satta.

Gesualdo Bufalino

THE KEEPER
OF RUINS

and Other Inventions

*Translated from the Italian
by Patrick Creagh*

HARVILL
An Imprint of HarperCollins*Publishers*

First published in Italy with the title *L'Uomo invaso*
by Bompiani editore, Milan, in 1986
First published in Great Britain
by Harvill
an imprint of HarperCollins*Publishers*
77–85 Fulham Palace Road,
Hammersmith, London W6 8JB

1 3 5 7 9 8 6 4 2

© Gruppo Editoriale Fabbri, Bompiani, Sonzogno, Etas S.p.A. 1986
Translation © HarperCollins*Publishers* 1994
Foreword © Isabel Colegate 1994

The Author asserts the moral right to be
identified as the author of this work.

A CIP catalogue record for this book
is available from the British Library.

ISBN 0 00 271017 X hardback
ISBN 0 00 271335 7 paperback

Photoset in Linotron Galliard by
Rowland Phototypesetting Ltd, Bury St Edmunds, Suffolk

Printed and bound in Great Britain by
Hartnolls Limited, Bodmin, Cornwall

Contents

Foreword

NOT LONG AGO a friend gave me a book with a fine mythological picture on the front called *Blind Argus*. I had never heard of Gesualdo Bufalino, but I read that he had been encouraged to publish his first book (*The Plague-spreader's Tale*), an account of his experiences in a tuberculosis sanatorium, by Leonardo Sciascia, whose work I did know and admire enormously, so I began to read in anticipation of finding something as deeply permeated with the atmosphere of Sicilian life and at the same time as clear, concise and politically acute as Sciascia. I found something very different. Bufalino is a wilder spirit, a more anarchic talent. At times he seems to be doing battle with a whirlwind of words which threatens to overwhelm him. Part of the pleasure of reading him when he is in this mode is just in seeing his tattered banner emerge victorious from the strife; but there are more sober moments, and gentler ironies, and the note of deep melancholy which underlies the exuberance is never far away. Certainly his imagination finds its roots in Sicily, where he has lived all his life in the same town, Comiso, between Syracuse and Agrigento in, as he is happy to claim, "the Greek part of the island". His is the Sicily of ancient myth and modern misery, the most desired and the most despoiled of Mediterranean islands, a place of vanished oak forests and valleys now arid which once ran with sparkling streams, plains which once grew corn for all of Italy and from which the god of the underworld stole Persephone, goddess of the spring, an island where at the awful moment of the fiercest noonday heat anything might happen, gods appear, individual identity dissolve, Empedocles leap into the heart of the volcano. It is also the land of superstition, poverty and pride, where of necessity much has always been kept dark. But to think of Bufalino as a regional writer in the generally understood sense would be to categorise him inaccurately, because his Sicily is also an island of the imagination, and his speculations fly too high to be chained to any particular rock.

Born in 1920, Bufalino was a schoolmaster, translator and local journalist until 1981, when Leonardo Sciascia persuaded him to publish the book which he had had in a drawer for thirty years or so and which he had written about his experiences in a tuberculosis sanatorium in Palermo after the war. The book was an instant success and won the Premio Campiello, an admirable award of which the judges comprise four hundred volunteer readers, chosen at random; *Blind Argus* and *Night's Lies* (which won another prize, the Strega) followed. Bufalino's publisher asked him whether he thought he could produce a book of stories, and he wrote the present collection of short pieces, fables, fantasies, meditations, imbroglios, all – even the slightest – expressive of that same imaginative world, in which the impulse to rejoice strangely survives the shocks of human existence, and the amazed apprehension of the world's beauty co-exists with a sharp awareness of its horror. Human passion leads to self-destruction, death and putrefaction are seldom out of mind, the simple are misled, the sincere are fooled, and as often as not the tragic is tripped up by the comic. Sometimes identities become unreliable; a man may be taken over by a seraph, another may lose his own memory and find he has gained someone else's, a puppeteer's apprentice finds himself being merging with his puppets, a private detective loses his sense of who is following whom. A dying man sees his own life as "a bedlam puppet show", death and imagination side by side in the same railway carriage. In quieter tales the old try to share what they know with the young, Eurydice, a sensible girl, knows only too well why the vain singer Orpheus turned to look at her, Noah, his voyage safely completed, wonders why his passengers, inheriting the earth, immediately begin to fight over it. Then there are the tales of intellectual frenzy which lead to madness as surely as do the lusts of the flesh; the monk whose role is to be the solitary guardian of the written wisdom of the world against the depredations of a deadly species of woodworm feels impelled to make the final sacrifice, the lonely reader maddened by the impossibility of knowing all that is knowable tries to make a miscellany of quotations and finds himself wandering the streets and bars of his home city laden with notebooks and pursued by a concatenation of imaginary voices raised in furious dispute.

The stories vary in tone and technique; as usual with Bufalino they must have been extremely difficult to translate. He himself has written "Your translator is the only authentic reader of a text. I speak not of critics, who have neither the time nor the inclination to get involved in such a bodily hand-to-hand struggle, but not even the author knows, concerning what he has written, more than an enamoured translator is able to guess at." Of no translator can this be more true than of Patrick Creagh who has been passionately engaged with Bufalino's use of language for many years. Anyone who enjoys words must enjoy Bufalino; but above all he leaves the reader with his own particular, and particularly vivid, sense of infinite possibility. Anything might happen, anything might be true; throw a question at the Universe and back will come the answer "yes". He has written, "God is better than he seems; Creation doesn't do him justice."

ISABEL COLEGATE

Being an Angel

FOR SOME TIME NOW I've suspected as much, though I just couldn't bring myself to mention it to anyone. But now the evidence stares me in the face: I, Vincenzino La Grua, am no longer a man but an angel, probably a seraph.

How this happened I have not the foggiest, but the proofs of my metamorphosis stand out a mile: they would convince a blind man. Although God knows how fond I'd grown of the mediocre flesh (sweaty palms, bad breath etc.) that has so far sheltered my existence. The human condition, with all its prickles, its tundras of yellow boredom, at least has this to be said for it: that it gives each of us a guarantee, signed by the mayor in person, of an indisputable identity; and while appointing us life-tenants of the cubic metre or so we occupy on earth, it does not thereby deprive us of the comfort of feeling at one with millions and millions of other far-flung human beings.

I wake in the morning and, so doing, am a brother to everyone else then opening his eyes in the world, owner like me of an odour, a face, a memory... Yet at the same time, if I go to the window and shriek "Vincenzo, Vincenzo La Grua!", not a soul down there looks up and thinks he is being called to. The syllables of the name I call belong to me and me only, to this humble, solitary, exclusive, inimitable 'I'.

Well, henceforth I shall have to get on without even such an indifferent certitude. A stranger has taken me over, and from now on it's a toss-up who 'I' may be.

But let's begin at the beginning. I had the first symptoms six

1

months ago in the bathroom. I was in the shower, chalk-white, teeth chattering. The hot water, for reasons unknown, having done a bolt, hundreds of icy jets were perfidiously assaulting me. I was therefore fumbling ineptly with the taps, precariously balanced on the edge of the bathmat, and suddenly lo! I no longer felt it under my feet, weightlessness emptied the marrow from my bones, and I levitated gracefully towards the ceiling. My first fear was of offending chastity, for this ascent would raise me, all white and naked as I was, to the level of the peep-hole that admitted light into the place, there to display my sparse black pubic hairs, with the risk that on the balcony opposite the lawyer's wife would quake with indignation for the innocence of her little girls.

Luckily it lasted only a moment or two. I found myself sitting on the floor, rather the worse for wear, unable to make out there and then whether I had risen saint-like in flight, or merely met with a *petit-bourgeois* accident such as can happen during any slippery Sunday morning ablution. . .

A few weeks later began the bleeding. Sneakily at first with small pinkish droplets, the stains of which I found on changing my vest, along the seams of the sleeves. But one midnight, returning by tram from a first night at the Opera (I'm a *claqueur* in my spare time – in my family we've always been musicians or singers or just plain opera-buffs) I felt a strange damp warmth on my shoulder blades, right and left, as if two springs of luke-warm lemonade had spurted from my back.

I alighted at the next stop, unbuttoned my shirt under a streetlamp, and tried to reach the double leakage with my fingertips: they came away red – the hands of a butcher's appren-tice. Back home, twisting my neck before the mirror, at the painful spots I descried two fresh ulcerations where the blood had clotted into scabs part glowing, part ashen, like the embers of an amputation. It crossed my mind, just to make a joke of it, that at one time, when I was in my cradle, they'd cut off my wings, and that now the stumps had decided to sprout again, as when children replace their milk teeth. Maybe those working sores heralded some sort of birth, and soon the down that covered them would burgeon into dense, birdworthy plumage...

With rather more reason, while getting undressed before slipping between the sheets, I reproached my wife Amalia for her caustic outpourings of the previous evening, and showed her the evidence behind my armpits. She protested, she scolded, I had to insist that these were not the brands and tokens of amorous sportings but something else again... Thereafter hints began to proliferate all round me: someone, it appeared, wanted to get over a message. The sword-hilt I discovered in the attic, for example, hidden in the thespian travelling-trunk my Uncle Hector had abandoned in 1949, after flopping as Manrico in Parma, could, admittedly, be simply the severed appendix of a stage sword; but all the same how rich and strange it was, with what phosphorescence did it flood the darkness! It seemed, even in the rags that swathed it, a barbaric trophy or ruby-studded diadem! And finally, one day, the Gustave Doré Bible, which I knew I had not leafed through for years, suddenly thrust itself upon me, open on the chest-of-drawers, and at the very page which speaks of Tobias and his mysterious travelling companion.

I began to get worried. An aberration had penetrated my body and I was unable to quell its fluctuations. One morning my hair fell out in sheaves, as if reaped by a scythe that brooked no denial; another morning it sprouted again, but soft, fine, wavy, of a blondness foreign to me. 'Angel's hair', Amalia called it, after an ultra-fine Sicilian spaghetti; and as she spoke she stroked it. Blandishments by this time unproductive. For towards women I had been waylaid by the most unbelievable impotence, while conversely I felt myself more and more the target of the lusts of others, both of dames and of damsels, who winked and brushed against me murmuring "Hullo, handsome!". But also of hirsute gentlemen, who pestered me in lifts and the bogs at railway stations. One of these persisted, fell on his knees, kissed my hand, implored me... I had to force him to his feet and solace him with a slap on the cheek.

I got a certain amount of fun out of this and other unusual portents. Not without a few blood-curdlers though. Like the time I discovered a heap of white feathers on the floor beneath the kitchen sink, and next to them, propped against the wall, a hatchet.

Now, I never weary of trying to reason things out – I don't allow myself to be rattled by first impressions. I am, as you will have realized, of temperate and domesticated habits, with virtually no leanings towards metaphysical sublimities. But if at daybreak for a week on end I chance to dream of a vast black icy space that suddenly disgorges an incandescent thunderbolt; if in my sleep I hear the beating of majestical wings on either side of the mattress, much like the rustle of leaves in a mighty forest; if I seem to rise with it higher and higher until I am leaning out over a dizzying sill, gem-set in the eye of God like a water-drop in the heart of an immortal flood; and if, more prosaically, now that June is upon us, I go up on to the terrace to acquire a tan, and realize that my bare feet are leaving prints that sizzle and steam on the tiles as if oozing spoonfuls of molten lead... Well I ask you, what am I supposed to think? What do you expect me to say?

I have made discreet enquiries around the place, and been to the library to do some research. The so-called Pseudo-Dionysius (I have the photocopy before my eyes) writes as follows: "Holy Writ speaks not only of fiery wheels, but also animals of fire and men, so to speak, shooting forth rays, and surrounds even celestial substances with heaps of burning coals and streams which with irresistible impetus send forth fire, and shows that the sublime Seraphim, in accordance with their name, are by nature scorching..."

So how do we stand? If I touch Amalia's arm with a fingertip it burns her; if I put a thermometer into my mouth it melts.

Amalia is sceptical, she brings everything down to her own level. "You always will go exaggerating," she tells me. "Everywhere you look you see miracles. You're even a bit fixated, if you ask me. Give you one slip in the bathroom, a couple of skin eruptions and a few goose-feathers you trod on in the kitchen, and you raise merry hell about it. For goodness' sake go and see the doctor. You just see if these so-called flames inside you aren't just flushes of hypertension..."

I lose my temper, wallop her one with a rolled-up newspaper and accuse her of being a deaf adder. She doesn't turn a hair, but flings in my teeth, "If you're really an angel, give me the numbers for a double in the Lottery!" So I laugh and give up. Though I do get my own back with the odd prank, such as scribbling a salacious imperative on the mirror with her lipstick, or appearing by night at her bedside dressed up in a dazzling white nightshirt and top-hat, to trumpet in her ear a hair-raising *Dies irae*.

Boyish tomfoolery, with which I seek to stave off graver thoughts and fears. Very well, I'm an angel, you can bet your buttons on that. But an angel being born, or born again? Am I undergoing a metamorphosis, or suffering an intrusion? Whoever is taking lodgings in my limbs, is he an unknown guest? Or is this some former and forgotten self reawakening in them?

When I chew these matters over as I lie sleepless beside a snoring Amalia, or, to our mutual embarrassment, I think them out loud between courses at lunch, I feel a lump in my throat and have to take my mind off it at once with a cigarette or a quick nip. The trouble I am in is now so patently obvious that my wife, however indirectly and maliciously, is beginning to see the light. The idea that I have been taken over no longer turns her stomach. In fact it quite perks her up, even if since she saw *The Exorcist* on the telly she favours a more exacting form of takeover. So much so that more than once I have caught her, on the pretext of wanting to clip my toenails, making a very close scrutiny of my feet, expecting (I imagine) to find a goatlike bifurcation. Likewise, whenever she sniffs the air and asks me if I've just struck a match, it is clear that in the room she detects, or pretends to detect, a whiff of sulphur. Nor do I care for the way that two evenings running she asked the local priest to dinner...

I, on the contrary, persist in the belief that whatever has infiltrated me is of wholesome quality. Even if I ask myself, why me? I'm just an ordinary bloke, I don't deserve visits from the nobs. My body is a modest dwelling, my sensibilities and intellect are of fairly low wattage. So I don't understand it. Unless perhaps the intruder is a spirit curious about the ways of the world, come to gain experience in any old workshop, as Heirs Apparent are packed off to be weaned on cruddy old corvettes or in border garrisons. Or else it might be a young scamp of an angel who's run away from school, like boys here on earth, jumping on the first train without a ticket and returning a month later hand in hand with a stony-faced constable.

I don't deny that I feel mistreated, violated, compelled to wrangle with some aggressive force to retain a scant remnant of myself. And then, what if Amalia were right, curse her! If I were indeed harbouring some petty Satan in transit, so cruel and silly as to make a pastime out of bedevilling the lot of a poor beggar like me...

Anyway, one thing is beyond dispute: I am suffering.

The last incident dates from the day before yesterday, and it clinches the matter.

I was prepared for it, but not so soon. The fact is that in recent times an ominous novelty has wormed its way into my language. I, who normally employ only decent, mannerly vocabulary, accompanied by temperate gestures, have – first at long intervals, then more often, finally every hour or half-hour – been seized by a kind of pornographic tic, and out pops some vulgar epithet, if not a downright obscenity. Therefore, when in company, like one who feels some unseemly eructation coming on, I have withdrawn with an excuse and rushed to the bathroom to spit the indecency into a coloured handkerchief pressed firmly to my lips. This has made my contact with the outside world both rare and arduous; it has counselled me to practise solitude. However, if there was one place where I felt safe from myself, that was the opera house. There (since we have the run of the place), to forestall danger I chose to take my stand behind a curtain, thinking that at the worst I would be able to restrain myself or, should the fit come on, disguise the fact.

Not this time. I had sneaked in while they were rehearsing one of those little-known titbits that appeal to me, the oratorio which Giacomo Carissimi devoted to the adversities of Job. I had two reasons for going: the first, one of tenderness and nostalgia, was to set eyes once again on Gertrude the Ticinese contralto, in my youth a passionate heart-throb of mine (have you ever paid due heed to these contraltos, such throaty, moody, unforgettable Messalinas?). And secondly, since there's an angel singing in this piece, to hearken to whether, as colleague to colleague, he didn't bring me some message from our Superiors. . . I can get on pretty well with Latin, and the same goes for quavers and demisemiquavers. So there I was, lapping up words and music with the greatest of pleasure and indeed, I confess, with a tear or two poised on the eyelid. But when, following the "*Audi, Job*", I heard the melody for the third or fourth time repeat, with infinite sweetness, its resigned, unruffled "*Sit nomen Domini benedictum*", I know not what convulsion of rage or of ridicule seized me, but I burst forth with an unthinkable blasphemy that drowned out singers and instruments alike, and hushed them on the instant.

I was manhandled and kicked out: the least I deserved. Then they had to call the loony-squad.

Here and now I'm well and happy. Amalia brings me in the newspapers, clean underwear, extra provisions. Not that the food here is bad, but I have set tastes and don't intend to change them. As for the rest of it, wholesome air, nurses middle-aged but attractive enough, gentle sedatives to be dissolved in water, a vase of flowers on the windowsill...

I bloom again. No dirty words ever pass my lips. I only think them. I constantly address the presence within me, but in the politest of terms. Speaking of which, I have had an idea. He must be an aborted creature doing all he can not to die, and sucking my human juices, usurping my memories, for this sole purpose: not to die. I shall have to get used to our living together. As friend and as foe. Reining him in or goading him on, as occasion demands. Domesticating him. I shall grow along with him, I shall be him, he will be me, we'll swap our vices and virtues back and forth. I already see myself, with his hand, guiding cripples and blind men through the whirl of the traffic, annunciating hallowed births from door to door with a lily in my fist; keeping vigil, a finger to my lips, before the bed-chambers of the dying; and at dawn one day, with flaming brand, slaying the dragon.

Eurydice's Homecoming

SHE WAS WORN OUT. As she would have to wait a while she sat down on a hummock near the river bank, within sight of the mooring-post where the boatman would make fast the painter. The air was the usual sulphureous yellow, like fumes from marl or volcanic ash, but greying on the shore into slack wisps of grimy tow. The light was dim, and it was cold, and the river itself seemed less to flow than to writhe in coils of pitchy paste, with snakelike sloth. A flicker of sudden wings, a flash of black, scored the surface of the water and vanished. The liquid closed over it in a trice, gulped it down. How had that bird found its way down here? Surely in the wake of the poet and his music.

"The Poet"... This was what she called her husband when they were alone together, when she wanted to provoke him, or else as a caress, when she woke at his side and saw him beating time to some new melody with great sweeps of his hand. "Are you making up a tune?" she'd say. But he didn't dream of answering, he put on such airs. And how precious and reassuring it was to her, that he gave himself airs, let his hair grow down on to his shoulders and forever set it to rights with the rush pen he wrote with. And didn't know how to boil an egg... Especially as he need only pluck a few chords and hum his latest hit to make everyone so peacefully, irremediably happy...

"...Poet!..." O now with more reason than ever! This time she murmured the word with a touch of umbrage: that scatterbrain of a poet, that adorable good-for-nothing... Fancy turning round like that, after so many warnings, only fifty yards from the light of day... She looked down at her feet – they were hurting her. If indeed that minikin of air, of which shades are made, can hurt.

What she felt was not disappointment but only a calm, regretful resignation. She had never in her heart believed she could really get out. From the first, the entrance – a one-way cul-de-sac, a shaft with iron-clad walls – had foreboded finality. This was death, no more and no less; and plummeting into it, at the instant she shuddered with horror at the viper's fang, she knew it was for ever: she was being born again, yes, but into darkness and for ever. She had clutched then at the frail straws of memory, clung to her own name that hung on a thread on the fringes of her mind, and Eurydice, Eurydice she cried again and again in the dizzying vortex as lower, ever lower, she went whirling down: Eurydice, Eurydice she cried, to add one mite of succour to the tiny coin hidden by his hand under her tongue at the burial rite.

> Are you dead, my life, and I still breathing?
> Have you then departed
> Never to return, and left me brokenhearted?

Thus had he warbled lyre in hand, and that monody had stirred her to the depths. She would fain have cried out her gratitude, cast loving looks upon him once again, but ah, she was nothing but an effigy of cold marble, with a slaughtered lamb at her feet, and laid on a pyre of arrogant brushwood. And no command that she strove to convey to her eyelids, to her ashen lips, unsealed them for an instant.

And what to tell of her new life? Of the new body she had been made to wear? Rarefied, shifting, evanescent as veils...

Things could be better, they could be worse. Those games of knucklebones and cards for two, girlish gossip with Persephone at her loom, and walks arm in arm along the byways of the kingdom, swapping confidences while Pluto slept, head swathed in a goatskin cap. It had all helped to while away the time, at least for half the year, and relieve the tedium of this garrison life. But tomorrow? And after?

She looked down at the water. On and on it came, ripple after ripple, like fishes' scales, to break against the bank. Grim and ancient water, brackish, putrid, swept by distant oars. She strained her ears: yes, the plop of the blades could be heard far off, striking the water at lengthy intervals. How sick of it he must be, that ferryman, forever to and fro, to and fro. . .

Thousands upon thousands of souls had gathered in the meantime, waiting. Even if she queued up it would be hours before her turn came. "Doesn't re-entry give one precedence?" she thought with a smile, though now that she had got this far she was in no haste to get back home. Thousands upon thousands were the waiting souls, shuddering with cold and squawking with a sort of famished eagerness. And that fire burning in the midst of them, it's a wonder how they had managed to light it, to kindle it at all: with what tinder-box, what pine cones? And they warmed themselves around it, for riverside air is noxious to naked bodies.

She smiled again: as if the dead still suffered from the rheumatics! Though she would dearly have wished to warm her hands at that flame, and to mingle the chirrup of her voice with the chirruping of the others. But she did not do so, she did not approach their fire; she preferred to be alone, to think. For a slight malaise, as after eating food that disagrees with one, ached beneath her ribs; and she knew it was not distress for the life she had lost twice over, for her resurrection gone awry. No, it was a different, an unwonted sourness, a regret unable as yet to become a thought, but pressing heavy within her like a babe unborn and rotting in the womb with neither name nor destiny. She knew not what to call it, an omen, a suspicion, a disgrace. . .

11

She retraced her whole story: she felt an urge to understand it.

Looking back on it, she had fallen in love with him late and reluctantly. At first she didn't fancy the way the other women ran after him – along with all the beasts of field and of forest. He must be a sorcerer, that man, a seducer of ears, a rapscallion to beware of. With that eternal lyre slung round his neck and his roving eye, and that glib patter of his... Then, one evening of much moonlight, finding herself in a wood, dreamily dreamily as her custom was, her feet taking her hither and thither reckless of the serpents lurking in the grass, into the thicket where she had sought a shadowy nest there crept a filament of music which moment by moment tautened, strengthened into an invisible cord that drew her towards it, enveloped her limbs, melted them on the instant into warm, soft honey, in a rapture and swooning like unto death. Nor did she awaken before the sensuous lips of the man, the vigour of him, had slowly withdrawn from her body.

She loved him then. They had a gala wedding – dish upon dish and pitchers of dark red wine. Marred only by one laughable little hitch: the torch which, though brandished lustily with both arms by Hymen himself, failed to catch and merely belched forth plumes of obnoxious smoke.

Thereafter followed halcyon days and nights. He could muster words none other could, and murmured them between her tresses into those twin pavilions of roseate flesh, in an arcane whisper, almost inaudible: and her whole being of a sudden stormed and thundered with love. A land of clouds and flowers was Thrace where they lived, and she remembered nothing else about it, no glade or heath or rocky hollow, but only clouds scudding across her vision and handfuls of petals torn from the ground in the instant of pleasure. With him she lay beneath a vast cup of sky, on a bed of leaves and wind, watching through tear-beaded eyelids the sway of the treetops, hearing the distant breakers dashing on the rocks or a roe deer belling in the thickets. She would dry her eyes with the back of her hand, reopen them. He would close them with a fingertip and begin to sing. "Already evening falls, and in the orchards the vesperal gold grows dark, and trembling cold in the viridian fingers of the araucaria the moon pours bounty from the mountains... Eurydice, Eurydice!" And she would lay her cheek on his breast and eavesdrop on the stirring of roots and the beating too, on the measured beat of an animal heart, or the heart of a god.

So, she had loved him. Even though she soon had doubts of being loved so well in return. All too often he slipped off to the heights of Rhodope with a band of youths with red ribbons about their wrists, or down towards the seashore, showing off with his retinue of bewitched nightingales, and himself bewitched by the songs begotten in him. Without a word about where he was going, or caring that he left her with nothing in the house, bereft of affection, exposed what's more to the salacious overtures of a neighbouring shepherd... If he had deigned at least to take umbrage, to make a scene. But not a hope! He confined himself, just for appearances, to intoning a lament about jealous love, which he forgot the next minute. When things are like this a woman loses interest, grows slovenly in her ways; and indeed of late she had neglected herself, gone about with matted tresses, carelessly got up, her skin scratched by brambles, chapped by mountain winds. And though she always told this Aristaeus "No, no and no again," she did so with less hauteur than formerly. Rather mildly, in fact, and from time to time even accepting a little spelt-cake or a posy of wild flowers. But then, no sooner did his cheekbones show a dark flush of wine or of lust, than she would flee. And so it was she died, as she ran from him, chancing with swift foot upon the strip of malice in the grass.

A curse upon the grass! And her thoughts turned anew to Persephone. A gem of a girl, but ill-starred. She too had brought trouble on herself by her love of wandering through the fields. A part-time friend, alas, but so lovely when she came back from her holidays, tanned and fit, with her arms full of springtime, bundles of white blooms, and amaranth, carnation, hyacinth. . . She wore them in her hair, the few hours they lasted, then put them in vases and insisted on sprinkling them with water from the Styx, can you imagine! She brought herself to throw them away only when they were really stinking. . .

Ill-starred maiden. Belovèd, albeit, of a husband and a mother. And one, moreover, who could afford to travel, to alternate asphodel with narcissus, the conjugal pomegranate with the fiery oranges of the upper world, to be at the same time frost and flame, blind socket and radiant eye, woman one and goddess threefold!. . .

An outcry brought her to herself. The barge had appeared abruptly, scudding over the waves as if from some last-minute punctilio on the part of a tardy oarsman, while on the bank the souls applauded and twittered and made imploring gestures, some of them waving flaming brands. Eurydice stood up to watch. The scene was, so to speak, infernal, with that vessel advancing over the lurid swell, and the reflection of flame on fog beneath which the rabble seemed to be writhing and proliferating, all straining forward, eager for the leap. In the batting of an eyelid the barge was brim full, so crammed that the passengers held their arms above their heads to make more room. A party of left-behinds attempted a last assault by latching on to a hawser. They fell back into the water, re-emerging laboriously, smirched with slime. There remained, forbidden to all, one place: a wooden bench beside the hoary old ferryman. "Eurydice," he hailed her. "Eurydice!"

She reopened her eyes. A tongue of icy water was lapping at her ankles. The barge was now at a standstill, rolling in mid-stream. Before her was the old man's bare, bent back, shaggy with white hairs. Through a hole in the planking a pool of water had seeped in, and he was stooping to bale out the bilge and caulk the leak. What an old tub! What tattered sails and how clumsily mended! "I was a lot handier with a needle," she thought. "I was a good wife to him. I loved that man, the poet. And all in all he loved me back. If not, he would never have wept such tears, taken such risks on crags, in crevasses, among tenebrous Manes and hosts of dreams with blackened talons; never have forded torrents, scaled escarpments, pacified monsters and Moirae, with no better armour than a linen mantle and a simple red ribbon round his wrist. Nor would he have distilled such sweetness of sound before the throne of invisible Pluto. . ."

The pressure in her side was painful now, but she was no longer afraid of it. She knew what it was – something that had slipped her memory, some single detail in her recent adventure, some trifle either seen or sensed or grasped in a flash, which the waters of Lethe had temporarily blotted out. A revelation, as it were, to be put away and remembered later. It would come back to her in a moment, of course, when that sip of Lethe, its potency waning, had wholly dispersed in the labyrinth of her veins. This was the law, even if she would have preferred total and everlasting oblivion to this flux and reflux of wakefulness and stupor, these temporary losses of awareness. . . As one who leaves his bed asleep and wakes on the brink of some parapet. . .

She thought again of her man, of their last encounter. With pride she thought of it. For the Poet had descended into these depths for her, for her had he forced those gates with a conqueror's tread, had subdued them all with the coercion of his song. Even Menippus, buffoon and jester that he was, had wiped the sneer off his face, taken his bald pate between his hands and wept among his bags of beans and lupin seed. And Tantalus had ceased to snap his lips at elusive drops of lymph, Sisyphus to roll his boulder with the main force of his paps. . . And Ixion's wheel, look you, idle in air, a hoop of derelict lead. A hero, a conquering hero, stood before them. Cerberus had crouched at his feet, licking those travel-worn sandals with triple tongue... And Pluto from his shrouding cloud had pronounced consent.

Once again she saw the sequel: the upward scramble behind him on that thorny, stony path, hobbling on a foot still throbbing with the venom of the asp. Glad at the sight of him, even if only his back; glad at the ban that would sweeten the delight of soon re-embracing him...

What Fury, what fatal wasp, had stung his wits? Why, why in his scatterbrained way had he turned round?

"Fare thee well, fare thee well!" she ought to have cried out after him, as she felt the golden wand of Hermes gently tap her shoulder. So she, sucked back by darkness, had watched him recede towards the fissure of daylight, vanish in a sunny dustcloud... But not without catching him, at that moment of heartbreak, sweeping his lyre-strings with eager fingers, touching them with professional zest... The air had not yet riven them asunder but boldly, confidently, came his voice:

"*Che farò senza Euridice?*"...

Nor did he seem to be improvising: "What avails life without Eurydice?" No, it sounded rehearsed at length before the looking-glass, with every one of those trills and grace notes, the whole thing ready for public performance, for the applause, the footlights...

The ferry was under way again, the jetty already just visible through the foul limp shreds of fog. The souls were hushed, serried together like cavern bats. Not a sound was heard but the slow, the solemn, dipping of the oars. Then felt Eurydice the blockage in her breast released, and triumphantly, woefully, she knew the truth. He had turned on purpose.

Gorgias and the Sabaean Scribe

SHORTLY AFTER HIS RETURN from Athens, Gorgias of Leontini resumed his habit of talking to himself. He left the city every morning, followed step by step by the young scribe he had received as a gift from Callicles, and exercised himself in lone and lengthy declamations. This scribe was a youth of swarthy hue, of simple heart and impulsive temperament, so solicitous of his new master as to dog him affectionately on these excursions of his, never giving him a chance to be alone and withdraw into himself. Hence Gorgias was by now resigned to seeing on the ground, beside his own, the shadow of the other, those noontides when the sun was at its zenith and every soul in the countryside was sleeping – all but the sentinels at the Fortress – and the trickles in the riverbed looked motionless, mere pools of molten light.

This was the hour the philosopher chose for his sorties outside the walls. Imprudently, it must be said, with so many Syracusan scouts in the vicinity; but then philosophers have never been known for their prudence. It was his custom to walk as far as the vast isolated carob-tree in the neighbourhood of Ceramia – such was the distance he required to elaborate a whole speech – haranguing the stones of the walls like some compliant audience and conducting the music of his voice with the snapping of his fingers. A curious man... For, had he not deserved the city's thanks for mediating the alliance with Athens and the support of Lachetes and his fleet, not all his magniloquence and air of inspiration and the intellectual sparkle of his eyes would

17

have availed to save him, along the way, from the scoffing of
the riff-raff.

As it was he was respected in the city, even admired, and
called upon to act as counsellor and ambassador in the most
desperate predicaments; but nobody loved him. Unless love
consisted of the doglike devotion of this young barbarian,
Sabaean by race, who leaving his native desert tribe had somehow landed up first in the service of Callicles and now of himself.
One who was hard put to it to speak our language, larding it
with impenetrable syllables from some unearthly idiom of his
own under the illusion that they had some meaning. But he
understood and wrote it to perfection. An ideal auditor, in
short, given that Gorgias required not opponents but accom-
plices, for he concerned himself less with capturing a man's
mind by main force than enchanting it, and delivering it, marvel-
ling, into bondage. With no weapon but the blade of his tongue,
no noose but his ravelled Gordian rope of speech.

"The spoken word," said Gorgias, wiping the sweat from his
brow with a handkerchief, "is a mighty dominator, which with
minimal and invisible substance can godlike feats perform,
allaying fear, assuaging sorrow, arousing joy, awakening
pity. . ."

They had reached the ancient tree and were seated cross-
legged beneath its shade. The youth had unwrapped their simple
repast of black olives and a pitcher of well-water, and subsequently a waxen tablet on which to record, as every other day,
whatever his master wished; though he entreated the sage to
help him maintain his calm by dictating slowly, so carried away
was he wont to be by that whirl of melodious concepts in
which now formed now faded, like a mirage among dunes, some
belittled, aggrandized, ever-debatable truth.

"Take, for example, Helen," dictated Gorgias, "whom the
poets never tire of reproaching for her effrontery, and of whom
Aeschylus says that she fled away down the paths of adultery

and brought to Ilium death for a dowry. Whereas I from the housetops dare to proclaim her innocent. For she acted as she did either by the decision of Chance, the will of the Gods, the law of Necessity; or else carried off by violent hands; or perchance induced by words of love. If the first motive be the true one the blame is not to be imputed to her, but rather to Chance, the Gods, Necessity; if the second, then the charge befits the author of the outrage, not her who suffered it; and finally, if she was led astray by the words and enchantments of love – whatever love may be, frenzy divine or malady of mortals – how then could you find it in your heart to condemn as unworthy a woman who acted under constraint and not of her own free will, who was not guilty but ill-starred? How could she be judged heinous on this account?"

Before that outstretched finger, stabbing him straight in the face, the servant became flustered. Called upon to act as judge, when he would have preferred to play the mere plauditor, he leapt to his feet crying "Divine Helen, you are the victress!" reddening the while and supplementing the name with some phrase babbled in his own language, in which Gorgias seemed to sense not only a verdict of Not Guilty but a surge of rapture and wholesome masculine ardour. He smiled, accepted the olive which the young man offered him, and chewed it exceeding slow.

A butterfly had meanwhile settled on his knee. Trustingly. Its wings iridescent with sunlight even though, on closer inspection, they sprouted from a wormlike body, grey, hairy, vile to the touch; like those of certain minuscule monsters which the hand disinters from beneath a rock, and from which are divined portents of disaster. A shudder of repugnance passed through the philosopher, sufficient for the insect to take fright at him, and abandon his knee to seek safety in a sunbeam. In vain did the serving-lad pursue its flight, or what he took for flight but was nothing but a glitter of fleeting dust; then he gave up and once more crouched down, stylus at the ready, waiting for the word.

It was then that he noticed the sandal. It was a bronze sandal that appeared to cling with some difficulty to his master's left foot; nor was it identical to its companion on the right, but merely similar. It had the same bronze sole attached by leather thongs, but was slightly broader and darker in colour, as far as could be distinguished from the rims and the interstices between the toes. A pitchy, smoky colour, as if it had been fired many hours in a blacksmith's forge, or come from the foot of a warrior struck by lightning.

The lad raised his eyes and looked a question at his master.

"It is a memento of my teacher," explained Gorgias. "All that was left when he was assumed into the fire. Ever since then I have worn it, for objects sometimes have better memories than men."

He leant confidentially towards his slave. He knew he would not be understood, but was glad to unburden himself to one who did not understand him, to an ear both deaf and loyal, in which unbeknownst to all he could conceal himself.

"Hearken to me," he went on therefore, in low tones. "But twice in my life have I suffered from envy, I who am the greatest of all, whose statue wrought in gold stands at Delphi like the statue of a god. But twice. The first time was for Empedocles, for knowing how to die. The second was for Socrates, this year in Athens, for how he lives and will one day know how to die. Socrates, you remember, you met at the house of Callicles. You several times brought him water, that day when his throat was parched from constant talking; and Callicles your old master was there himself, and that young chatterbox Polus, and a silent young fellow whose name I don't remember. And I spoke of my art, of the purpose of this art which I profess, the art of persuasion... Well then, what I did not say that day, what I did not dare to confess, is that this treasure I possess, here at the tip of my tongue, this my majestic rhetoric, is but a puff of wind which stirs the treetops, seeming to subject them to its will, but which soon dies down while they once more arise,

20

motionless against the cerulean of the sky. Whereas dying, knowing how to die, that is the one thing which justifies us here on earth. Now, I know that I shall die at a great age. Empedocles predicted this of me, and he was an infallible sooth-sayer and miracle-worker. Once I saw him resuscitate a woman who had lain thirty days on her bed without drawing breath. Yes, I know that I shall die very old, but I have fears of not knowing how to die; that my rhetoric, at the moment of passing, will be powerless to conjure up either the silence of Empedocles or the speech of Socrates. . ."

The lad was no longer writing, but listening. Still impassioned and happily uncomprehending, but curious about that black-ened sandal.

"It is his last message; who knows what secret it has to tell. . ." speculated Gorgias under his breath. He removed the sandal and held it in both hands, examining it like an archaeological find. And indeed that erupted bronze was as if begrimed with a thick deposit of lava, scratched like all *lapilli* with hieroglyphics wrought by the mysterious hand of fire.

The butterfly now all of a sudden returned to Gorgias, dodging his hands and perching on the tip of the sandal, in the likeness of a gem or the petal of a flower.

"Hush!. . ." His stern look checked the youth as he started to rise and resume the chase. "It may be *him* returning. . ."

"Him?"

"Empedocles. Returning. For he in his time was boy and girl and shrub and bird and darting fish in the sea. He wished to die to hide himself in things, and from them to rise again a god. Why, pray, should he not have changed himself into a butterfly? I know how much he cherished the most volatile of states. . ."

It was not the first time the slave had heard Gorgias speak of his teacher, how he would stalk through the streets of Agrigento clad in purple, his brow begirt with sacred fillets and crowned with flowers, and mothers in their doorways calling out to him

to heal their ailing children, and peasants to protect them from
foul weather, and how once he imprisoned the wind in donkey-
skin bottles and they called him "the gaoler of the wind". . . The
serving-lad knew all of this, but it did his heart good to hear it
all over again and he drank in the discourse of Gorgias as if it
were a fairy-tale. But not without perceiving that it was infused
with such deep gloom as comes to a bereaved disciple who, to
heal his bereavement, consents to become teacher in his turn. . .

"Concord and Discord," resumed Gorgias, "govern the world.
This he taught me, this I teach to you. Nor does the one exist
without the other, nor ever fully prevail over the other. Yesterday
you saw heads sprout neckless from the earth, and roving arms
bereft of shoulders, and eyes drifting alone, detached from brows.
But behold today the scattered parts reassemble to form this
paltry human engine we call ours. Brief, however, is its lot.
And so meagre a part of life is it fitted to discern. . ."

He rose, fixing his gaze on an invisible army of shades. "Ye
men," said he. "Ye like smoke in the air dispelled, the little ye
meet with ye believe is knowledge, and persist in believing that
it is the whole. . ."

He had hung the sandal by a thong on a stub of branch and
remained thus, half shod, rubbing the bare foot on the ground
as mules will their hoofs. The butterfly had once more flown
away; nor did he seem to remember it.

He swept his arms in a vast circular gesture that encompassed
and embraced the heavens, the growing grass, the river waters,
the warmth of the sun.

"All this!" he said. And a tear welled from his eye, coursed
slowly down his cheek, stopped on his chin by a tuft of hair.
"The birth and death of this. . . And our exile, the accursèd
severance. The birth that severs, the death that reunites. And
us, me, you, everyone, torn limb from limb and banished from
the kingdom of the Gods, fugitives on the pathways of this
world, and ever thus, to all eternity, guilty of having espoused
the madness of Discord. . ."

He dried his cheek with a finger, said: "Boy, give me a sip of water now."

The whistle of the arrow might have been the twitter of a swallow. Struck fair and square, the pitcher shattered, splashing its modest contents over the nearest boughs and spattering the philosopher's tunic. He was left with shards in his hand and stupefaction on his face. The slave shot to his feet with a yelp of terror, turned to shield his master's body with his own, and both of them backed against the rough trunk of the tree. Not a soul to be seen. Out beyond the dark green shade of the tree nothing met the eye but the stubble-fields of the plain lit with scudding dapples of sunshine. Not a living thing, all the way to the horizon. Except that from some distant cover came a flash: helmets surprised by the sun as it swapped one cloud for the next. Then the archers emerged into the open and advanced upon the pair.

There were only a few of them, just a patrol, and they came peering about them, suspicious lest our friends might not be alone, but the visible spearhead of an enemy outpost. They approached slowly, therefore, bows at the ready and with anxious faces. When they reached the tree one of them laughed aloud. "Bless my soul, the philosopher!" said he. "A good catch and an easy one. An unarmed chatterbox. It's Gorgias."

Gorgias knew the man. "Hermocrates," he hailed him. "They've given you a very puny army to command. Is that all the Syracusans think of you?"

Hermocrates scowled. He was young: on his powerful neck-muscles he tossed a mane of long black hair. But his soldierly mettle cut two precocious furrows at the corners of his mouth.

"You, go in peace," he said to the scribe. "And you, Gorgias of Leontini, come along with me. Though perhaps I ought to call you Gorgias of Athens, since you so fawn on that city beyond the seas. You'd have done better to stay there. Sicily is too uncouth for you. . ."

Gorgias had recognized him at once, for some years earlier, before the two cities came to blows, they had been table-companions and had talked at length at symposiums on the Acradinas.

"Come with you? Why not?" He smiled at the servant and, with a glance at the sandal hanging on the bough, "It's yours," he said. "Along with this other one." And he shook the remaining sandal from his right foot. "You are a free man. Go!"

Thereupon, barefoot and light-hearted, surrounded by the four archers off he went. But the servant ignored instructions. Mumbling and grumbling he followed in their wake.

Their destination was a little cave, where the Syracusans had slept the night before and the stones of the camp-fire still retained the heat of the flames. A few dry twigs were enough to make it catch again; and they ate, they drank, they talked. The cave was small, perched above the gorge of the Alcantara, whence arose a murmur of water that seemed to repeat one single somnolent undying phrase. The five of them sat round the fire and chatted, while of the servant, in the darkness, they had lost all trace.

"So then, you are my prisoner," began Hermocrates. "It goes against the grain, but I have to do it. After all, you betrayed the island to the advantage of the Athenians, you even summoned them in arms against us!"

Gorgias raised one hem of his mantle, covered his face with it for a moment, then looked back into the firelight.

"For prisoner you have taken nobody," he smiled.

"I'm not a Cyclops, for you to fool me with your Nobody," retorted Hermocrates heatedly. And he grasped the other's arm.

"No, Hermocrates, I mean it. And you who fancy yourself as a philosopher can follow the thread of the argument. For you to have me as your prisoner I must needs be someone, and

24

my being must be something other than non-being; and it is needful above all that being indeed should *be*. . ."

"You can't take me in," sneered Hermocrates. "You exist all right and I'm touching you. My spear isn't tickling a ghost. . ."

And he jabbed the spear against the other's flank. Very gently, but the stuff of his garment ripped and a drop of red coursed slowly down the philosopher's leg.

"One of three things," proceeded Gorgias, unheeding. "Either being is engendered and finite, or unengendered and infinite, or engendered and unengendered at the same time. In the first case it would be engendered from that which is not, that is, from nothing. You can see for yourself how absurd is the very concept. In the second case, were it unengendered and infinite it would have no limits in time nor find any place that could contain it. You can see for yourself how far existence may be attributed to that which at no point whatever, either in space or time, is. Finally, how can a thing be at one and the same time both engendered and otherwise? Are you not pained by such a contradiction in terms?"

Hermocrates laughed again. "Have it your own way, but if you are nobody I, equally, am nobody. Therefore permit nobody to amuse himself by killing nobody." And he thrust the metal a little deeper into the other's flesh.

Gorgias shrugged. "Kill me? As if nature did not already decree my death, and yours, and everyone's, with a decree manifest to every mortal, on the very day we came into the world. If indeed you wish to call it death, and not, rather, a separation of parts. For you see, nothing of what appears is simple: all is confused, composite, intermingled, death with life, Zeus with Hera, Nestis with Aidoneus. And right partakes of wrong, falsehood of truth, beauty of ugliness, evil of good. This is the tragedy and the wonder of our being-nonbeing here on earth. This it is my eloquence proclaims and sings. My words by turn dissever and reconcile opposites, flashing now this now that before the eyes, as occasion offers, so that great things seem

25

small and small things great, the old seems new, the new seems old... And not without an inner music to ensweeten the mind..."

Hermocrates did not hear him. Some time since he had blocked his ears with two wax pellets and confined himself to watching him from the far end of the cave, where a rough bed had been thrown together. But Gorgias did not fall silent on this account, but continued to discourse in that same manner of his, nurturing the secret rhythm of his oration, coiling every syllable skilfully into the next or leaving it there voluptuously to languish.

When the time came to sleep arrangements were made for guard duty, with two-hour watches, each man in turn to take over from the other outside the cave. A piece of military ingenuity that was to shame Hermocrates for the rest of his life. For Gorgias' slave, crouched in the darkness, felled the three of them one after another as they emerged, tottering with sleep, to relieve their fellows. A swift, light-footed shadow, he caught them unawares from behind, armed only with a bronze sandal sturdier than a hammer.

When at first light Hermocrates awoke, having reserved the last watch for himself, his own spear was pointed at his throat. Standing above him, looming above him (who would have thought he was so tall?), was the scribe with spear in hand and in his eyes a serene triumph, while the philosopher, also awake and on his feet, was leaning against the cave wall observing the scene.

"Hermocrates, you are my prisoner," he parodied, helping him to his feet. But he could not but nod assent when the Syracusan, rubbing his sleepy eyes, replied: "Gorgias, for prisoner you have taken nobody."

Gorgias and his servant started back to Leontini. Hermocrates, by his consent, had already left them. The philosopher walked briskly, now that he had recovered his footwear. Saddened though, and silent at last, at the thought that some had perished on his account and that he bore the smell of them, on the sole of his sandal, in clots of black blood and hair. At length he turned to the servant. "Servant," said he. "I will keep my promise: you are a free man. From now on you will live in my house as a friend. But tell me, by what name would you have me call you, in exchange for the name once yours in the freedom of the desert?"

"Empedocles," replied the scribe. "Call me Empedocles." And with a smile he opened his fist, displaying a butterfly impaled on a stylus.

Two Nights in the Life of
Ferdinand I

First Night

ON THE EVENING OF April the 25th 1824, eight months before his death, Ferdinand I of Bourbon*, by the grace of God King of the Two Sicilies, of Jerusalem etc., Infante of Spain, Duke of Parma, Piacenza, Castro etc. etc., Hereditary Grand Prince of Tuscany etc. etc. etc., afflicted with rheumatism and gout in the right leg, though still a top-notch shot and horseman, went to bed in his country residence at Persano at the end of a carefree day in the woods.

He had no reason to fear a bad night, for as a rule he fell asleep without any trouble, even when he had lost a hundred or even two hundred chips at cards to General Naselli or the Prince of Roti, Don Giuseppe Capece Minutolo. Ferdinand, as we know, was a man of strong bodily impulses but mentally sluggish and sensual, ostentatiously convinced of his royal prerogative, never doubting that his kingdom was simply a vast game reserve in which wild boar and subjects alike browsed merely with a view to offering themselves to his gun or the

---

* Ferdinand IV of Bourbon, King of Naples and thereafter King of the Two Sicilies, with the title of Ferdinand I, had an adventurous life. Expelled by the French Revolution, he was returned to the throne with the aid of the Royal Navy which, under the command of Nelson, enabled him to put down a republican uprising. Among those executed was the valiant Admiral Caracciolo, whose death was said to have been urged by Nelson out of jealousy of the former's prowess as a seaman; and Nelson, it is said, was instigated to this by Lady Hamilton.

caprices of his clemency. A hulking, self-satisfied fellow, with a few unexpected outbursts of whimsicality and humour whenever the prankster Punchinello within him woke up for a moment and spoke in his ear. There was therefore no earthly reason for him to fear a bad night. Nevertheless, after getting into bed at half-past ten, he endured several troubled and puzzling hours, "having continuously dreamt the most extravagant things", as he wrote the following morning to his second wife, the Duchess of Floridia. And these are reticent words, unusual in an effusive person accustomed, when writing, to giving a meticulous account of every gastronomic blow-out and subsequent evacuation. But this time, whether the visions had come to him so pell-mell as to prove indecipherable, or whether he was checked by some instinctive restraint, the fact is that he went no further than that bare hint; thus authorizing us – after the manner of philologists who labour to patch up the lacunae in a papyrus – to make good his silence and to conjecture, for example, that he that night part dreamt, part fancied in half-sleep, the following gallimaufry of death and happiness.

He dreamt he was in Sicily one mid-August day of twenty-five years before, immediately after his sanguinary voyage to Naples for the summary trials. The previous evening he had eaten and drunk unstintingly in honour of the birthday of his consort, Maria Carolina, while the festivities in honour of Santa Rosalia, graciously postponed so as to take place on the return of the royal voyagers, were imminent in the city. He had drunk too much, to the point of treating Lord Nelson to one of his characteristic gaffes, accompanied by a bellow of laughter and a loud sneeze. "My dear Duke of Brontë," he had said, "what a shame you're missing an eye and an arm, because with Lady Hamilton a chap needs four eyes, four arms... In a word, double everything!"

Nelson gave no sign of having heard; he merely paled slightly.

Then, raising his eyeglass to his blind eye, "I see you not, Your Majesty," he murmured. "Truly I see you not." Whereupon he turned his back and walked off. One-eyed, lop-limbed Englishman! Would he were not such a pet of the Queen's, and so useful to the tottering fortunes of the Throne! An insolent deckswabber who couldn't make port in a storm off Palermo without the help of a Bourbon officer. And as for sailing against the wind he couldn't hold a candle to Admiral Caracciolo.

Caracciolo... A corpse, erect and swollen, began to bob up and down behind his eyelids, plunging and surfacing in the black waters of the Gulf: an unsinkable tumbler-toy, round its neck the purplish marks of a noose, its blue eyes staring. What a strange thing – that though they were closed, you could still see the colour... Then near that head a hurly-burly of others that swarmed and thronged the scene, a round-dance of dead-men's heads, plunging and surfacing and fixing him with expressionless gaze: the head of Antonio Ferreri, the court courier, torn to pieces by the mob beneath the very windows of the palace; the head of that woman Sanfelice, her hair sticky with blood, a livid, waxen rose on the floor of the basket; Michele Morelli and Giuseppe Silvati, a brace of heads...

The king moaned, murmured I know not what, and turned over in his sleep.

Now he finds himself in a place full of greenery, with great clouds passing overhead. He recognizes the box-tree walks, the holm-oaks, the palm-trees of "La Favorita", his pleasure-gardens. Venanzio Marvuglia the architect lays out his drawings as best he may on a bench, lifts a hand to straighten his hair, ruffled by the sirocco, explains, asks questions, answers them himself. The king is not listening to him, but looking absently this way and that. Monte Billiemi is veiled in blue shadow but the sunlight, a blackish, scorched sort of sunlight, is oozing over the eroded gullies of Monte Pellegrino like cuttlefish-ink sauce. The air is sultry, and Ferdinand clicks his tongue noisily against his palate, a signal which the footman interprets in a flash. From a cloth he unwraps a copper jug full of pure water from the Garraffello and pours it into a glass of clearest crystal. There was only the one glass: Marvuglia can sweat to his heart's content.

The king looks up at the mansion rising before his eyes, trying to distinguish the outline from the forest of scaffolding. The voices of the workers on the high platform reach him attenuated by the wind. One voice, bolder than the rest, can be heard singing Meli's verses on the fall of the Neapolitan Jacobins:

> *Sagra Real Famiglia,*
> *la cosa è già finita,*
> *sta Libertà abbatuta,*
> *paura 'un ci n'è cchiù.**

A tribute to the sovereign, of course, even if the lad makes himself heard at the cost of leaning perilously out from a wobbly plank. Well done, young fellow, well done. The king applauds from a distance and draws a contented breath. He is happy to be alive, to be king, on a morning as light as the flight of a lark; he is happy not to have to sign death sentences today, to be able to concede his heart this armistice in a place so verdant, before a house even now growing up, like a child who in girl-hood already foreshadows a poignant and sinuous beauty. A gifted devil, this Marvuglia. He must be lavishly paid. A pity he's not Neapolitan, because these Sicilians... Carolina is right to find them nauseating. A people with hearts full of vipers and sophistries. Arrogant! Impulsive! Like that Friar Diego, years ago, who strangled the inquisitor! And the other one, whatsis-name, Valla, Villa, it's on the tip of his tongue... At any rate, that abbot from Malta (Sicilians, Maltese, they're all of a kind) with those fake Arabic manuscripts of his... And last but not

---

* "Holy and Royal Family,/ all is over and done with,/ this Liberty is vanquished,/ and fear there is no more."

least Giuseppe Balsamo, that fiend Cagliostro, the devil take him... The king mutters in his sleep. A bad lot, the Sicilians. Downright cannibals. But what a sky they have! And what a sea! What's more they love their king. Like that youth singing:

> *Cantamu tutt'a coru,*
> *tutti allegri gridannu:*
> *Evviva Firdinannu,*
> *l'invittu nostru re!**

The lad ought to be more careful, though. Can't think why Master Marvuglia doesn't tick him off. But Marvuglia's only thoughts are for eulogizing the building; he never stops talking and singing its praises from cellar to cornice: "This is the belvedere, with *such* a heavenly view... On the ground floor, here is the ballroom, and over here the audience chamber... All decorated in different styles – the Pompeian, the Turkish, the Chinese – and more magnificent than anything yet seen on the face of the earth... Where are the statues, do you ask? All in due time. Why not commission one from Canova – a prosopopoeia of His Majesty in the person of Minerva Pacificatrix?"

At this the king laughs. A droll notion, dressing him up as a woman, and Minerva at that... Minerva would do better for Carolina, if anyone, although Carolina would incline more towards Venus...

The king laughs even louder, and counts on his fingers the number of "finesses", as he calls them in his mental notebook, tried out in the queen's arms during the last week. From now on he had better keep a tight rein on himself at home if he wished to be on good form for his forthcoming amorous encounters elsewhere... There's that Princess Partanna, for instance, flesh of milk and honey, far-famed eyes... As long as

---

* "Let us sing all in chorus,/ all crying out for joy,/ Long Live Ferdinand/ our unconquered king."

Don Venanzio remembers to equip the first-floor bedroom with a secret escape-route. . .

Cantamu tutt'a coru,
tutti allegri gridannu. . .

Isn't that lad ever going to stop?

Evviva Firdinannu,
l'invittu nost. . .

A scream, a thud, a plank rotating negligently in space: will it never reach the ground? But swifter, flailing blind arms in the air like scarecrow's wings, swifter plummeted a body, to sully the thigh of a white satin trouserleg with a spurt of scarlet.

Second Night

The night of January the 3rd 1825 Ferdinand I went to bed in a bad mood. Partly from chagrin and remorse at having the previous day received a notorious jinx, one Canon Iorio, and partly due to rheum in his nose and chest that would not respond to treatment. He told his chamberlain, Don Carlo Ciavarria, to leave him alone the following morning, not to come and wake him as usual at the crack of dawn. Then he put on his long nightshirt, pulled the blankets about him and blew out the two-branched candlestick which kept him company. He never caught a wink: the catarrh and the coughing gave him no respite. And in addition to the discomforts of the body he was vexed by a rambling of the mind, a jumble of lost faces and voices, as always happens to an old man unable to sleep.

How long had he been king? Sixty-five years? Seventy? He had begun as a child scarcely able to read. And since then numberless summers and winters had passed, days happy and unhappy. More of the latter perhaps? Not a bit of it! Instead of counting sheep he tried recollecting his happiest moments. He'd had some good times, by Jove, and it took but a spark beneath his eyelids to rekindle them. Travels, balls, hunting-parties, mistresses, . , And his revenges, retributions, sovereignly acts of clemency... A sea of lights, a pageant of bygone hours blazed up in the night. What a puppet-show his life had been, like the playhouse in Palermo, in Piazza Marina, where he went incognito so many years ago to see the great Marotta in the role of 'Nofriu the porter...

A pain started up at the base of his skull, softly; a soft, painful growth that from thence stretched its branches inwards; but tentatively, as if uncertain which direction to take.

Women... He thought of women. How many of them, court ladies, country wenches, ballerinas from the Teatro San Carlo, plump as quails, voluptuous as doves...

He thought of his travels. Travels by land and sea, through snow-capped mountains and on broad, far-stretching highways. The north wind soughing in the rigging of the *Vanguard* mingled in his ears with the creaking of a litter on the hazardous passes of Leybach.

He thought of the evenings at cards, at piquet, primero, and all the bawling amid the clink of coins and glasses. At midnight the liveried footmen would arrive with fresh candles, while every so often Maria Carolina peeped in at the doorway... Off with her! Carolina positively brought him bad luck. It spelt trouble if she dared to enter his presence during a game without covering her face with a fan!

But the pain was now on the march: it seemed to have taken a decision. It was as if an army of tiny millipedes were trampling along under his scalp. It was on the march, and lord knows where it was aiming for. But all those diamonds, those rubies... What delight it had been to see them glittering there, in the sombre bed of a casket, a gift in readiness. Jewels, precious

34

things... He remembered, he made an effort to remember, the treasure he took with him on his first sea-voyage: fine furniture, crown jewels, all the loveliest things in the realm. He remembered the mirrors, the silks, the perfumes, the porcelain. And he relived the feeling of leaning out from a balcony above an ecstatically crowded mall, as the iron-shod clamour of racing Barbary steeds receded over the cobbles.

Now the armies of pain had picked their camp-site and were digging in...

How young he was when, after a shooting-party, he had totted up the bag – hare, pheasant, partridge, woodcock – before going off to cry his wares in the market like any barrow-boy! To be a good shot takes a good eye. Game must be hit at the wing-joint, not in the belly. A lesson never to be forgotten by the Prince of San Cataldo, who from that day forth never showed his face at one of the king's shoots!

The king stared wide-eyed into the dark. How many dead! And he himself, how lonesome. But thank God that cough had gone. The pain was still there, though, condensed into a sort of refulgent globe, a chandelier with a thousand flames in a whirl of dancing things. He dozed off for half a minute, and then it was he saw the greasy pole, such as you find at fairs, which the country people try to climb to get a shower of sweet-meats – or of cinders. More than once he dreamt he was scaling it himself, but each time his hands and legs lost their grip and he felt himself falling, as the singing builder's boy had fallen that noon at "La Favorita". Was that fall, that defeat, the image of his life, he wondered?

And history: what would history say of it?

The pain suddenly became unbearable.

Poor foolish history... A blood-vessel broke in his head. He heard, just before hearing no more, a tearing behind the eyes, like gauze slashed with a knife... Then through a thousand entries he was stormed and swamped by a great wave of darkness.

Don Carlo Ciavarria had heard the king cough twice at about six in the morning. At eight, not seeing him rise, he knocked discreetly. Receiving no response, he made so bold as to enter.

The king – as reported by Pietro Coletta – was lying in a jumble of sheets and blankets, entangled so bizarrely that he would seem to have had a long struggle. One sheet was wrapped round his head, and this bundle in turn hidden beneath the pillow; the legs and arms contorted; the face blotched ashen and black; the eyes gaping and terrible to behold; the mouth open as if to cry for help or drag in his last gasp of air.

The Death of Giufà

OF TALES ABOUT GIUFÀ* I know no end. Like the time he
sold a length of duck-cloth to a statue... Or when his mother,
leaving for church, told him to boil up a bean or two, and he
took her at her word and put just two in the pot. Then, testing
them for salt, he ate them both... Or the night he was guarding
the barn from thieves, chattering away and answering his own
questions, and they took him for an army of mounted police,
and ran for it...

I shall now relate the manner of his death.

Giufà blinked his eyes, then shut them. He'd feel less hungry
that way. He had long known the secret of putting hunger to
sleep – ever since first, as a boy, he had felt it like an animal
crept inside him, a little vixen nibbling at his innards that he
could stave off by whistling to himself, or humming a lullaby.

> Go to your slumbers, Giufà go to bye-byes,
> This child is a-weary and wants for to sleep...

until the encumbrance of slumber lay heavy on his head, a hood
of inky blackness occasionally pierced by flashes of vision, now
a pot of beans, now a salt anchovy, now a prickly-pear to pluck

---

* Giufà, in Sicilian folklore, is emblematic of the complete simpleton, though
capable at times of acting with craft and low cunning.

in passing – 'ware of the prickles! – with a hand as artful and
calloused as an old man's...

And so for years and years he lived on air. But now he is
really an old man, is Giufà. No trick of fancy can beguile the
grey fox gnawing at his vitals...

So Giufà, what's keeping you? Didn't you hear the squawking
from a nearby hen-run, close by just over the wall? What about
that enticing clucking there in the darkness?

Giufà slips from his hide-out. From what can be seen through
the tiny hayloft window it is still pitch dark. The hour when
in the farmhouse all are still sleeping, the hour propitious to
purloiners of poultry, but Giufà makes cautious headway, one
step, two steps, straining at the knee and breathless in the chest.
How long has he endured this vagrant life, all up and down
and crawl around, on the sheep-tracks eating the dust, at the
drinking-trough drinking like the pigs, snatching cat-naps that
you never knew when to snatch or when some peasant's pitch-
fork won't puncture them just at the best part... How many
years? He ties his fingers in knots in his efforts to count. They
must be more than threescore years, Giufà's: he was a lad when
Garibaldi came by, an almost beardless youth when he saw
Salibba the bandit shot down among the cork-trees, a cherry-
wood stick in his hand, and a dog at his side which licked the
blood from his face... Yet all in all it hasn't been a bad life, the
way he's had to live it, from season to season in sun and rain,
frosty mornings, sweltering noons, in country barnyards and
village alleyways, and a host of human voices whispering in his
ear even now, friendly-like. What a tender sound has the human
voice, what a tender concert is life, played by a band of
thousands upon thousands of instruments, flutterings of wings,
purlings of brooks, the night-wind in among the houses...
a concert of rustling, bellowings, pantings, whimperings; a
concert of man and of beast, of land, sea and air, a concert
that in the end is simply the music, the ineffable music, of

living. . . It is only the stars that make no sound, twinkling and bloodless up aloft, resembling the gems round the neck of the Madonna Addolorata when she rears and rocks above the heads of the mourning crowd like a fishing-boat ploughing the waves.

They say he's simple-minded, Giufà, but that isn't true; or at best it's true half-way. It's simply that he trusts completely in the face-value and guilelessness of words. If they name a thing, to him they mean just that, no more and no less. Without the misleading trappings with which man has cloaked them over the centuries. So that when he is told to boil up a bean or two, two beans it is; when he is reminded to pull the door close behind him when he leaves the house he obeys with a will, and pulls and pulls until he has torn it from its hinges and dragged it away. . .

The same with causes and effects: he sees only stitch by stitch, while the whole fabric escapes him. If he takes the ass to drink and sees the moon reflected in the pool then suddenly vanish from sight, he blames the ass for having drunk it and beats it until the moon sails free of its cloud and is shining once more in the water. So, "I told you I'd make you spit it out!" he brags to the ass.

Ah, the heartless mockery of youth! These are yarns the girls swap out of girlish silliness, for a laugh, as they sit in their doorways weaving rush seats for chairs. And if they see the old man go by in his raggedy uniform, a soldier without an army, they call to him, the little minxes, they egg him on with talk of love and kisses, and at the end, to make up for it, they give him a sesame cake or a honey-bun. Scarcely enough to stave off the pangs for an evening, let alone spare him having to return on the morrow to his eternal forays against field-guards and farmers. Never suspecting that field-guards and farmers have long since turned a blind eye to his trampish pilferings, and let him maraud undisturbed through the kindly blindness of the night. . .

Like tonight, when all have stayed up to wait for the Big Race to go by, the race that anyone who can read has seen billed on every stuccoed wall from Termini to Buonfornello. Along with the most thunderous warnings not to allow stray calves or unattended children on the highway, not to lean out at corners in the path of the hurtling vehicles, but to have bandages to hand for the injured and succour in the form of bread and wine for the army race-stewards on bicycles.

Giufà cannot read, and knows nothing of the race. His consciousness is entirely focused on a plump hen and a warm egg there in the darkness. Towards these, laboriously, he crawls, pausing more frequently the nearer he draws to the hen-coop. His heart does a drumroll as he spies a farmhand outlined against the sky, an unexpected apparition in homespun hunter's outfit, a shotgun on his forearm and a water-bottle slung over his shoulder.

Half an hour passes; to Giufà it is like playing hide-and-seek. Then the man rides off on a mule. He must act fast now, make the most of the truce. A ribbon of softer blue on the brink of the horizon means most of the night is gone. Quick now! Two more spurts, a few steps at a time, and then the last – an eternity! – and a gasp of exhaustion and relief. It's as good as done: his fingers will be swift, silent, deadly as ever.

Now it is no longer night, but not yet day. On the sea, rounding the rocky needle of Punta Scorsona, great sails are spread in the wanness of pre-dawn like drab archangels' wings. Scarcely visible to the eye, so besmirched with brine and fog do they rise and fall low over the water. Giufà is taking a breather behind a bank of brambles, with three eggs in a handkerchief and his shirtfront sagging with the weight of a strangled guinea-fowl. As he rests he thinks, and into his thoughts come distant figures, the girls of his youth, when they used to walk out in pairs, their twill capes clasped tight about them, twittering like sparrows; and others, of riper years, shooting glances sharp as cobblers' knives through the chinks in their shawls. The widow Arcidiacono comes to mind, for example, that evening when she beckoned him in to sickle the weeds round her gate, and afterwards drew him by the hand, and wanted him in the house, on top of her, and even gave him an ounce of silver. A naked white she-devil: Giufà trembles even now at the thought of her, though with a swoon of sated pleasure in his blood, remembering that sheen of flesh, fat and white in the bed like a cow, majestic in the wedge of moonlight entering through the skylight, while his eyelids were falling shut on him, "Go to your slumbers, Giufà go to bye-byes", and she was babbling away and kissing his face all over and drumming little punches on his back. . .

What a moon that night over Girgenti, what a moon. . .

Now the old man Giufà is stretched out behind a hedge and knows not how to pass the time, now that he has reviewed the whole jubilean charter of his life. In the lull before dawn the highway beyond the hedge is invisible, though it seems peopled, and battered by strange hoofs. Something heavy, who knows what, every so often causes it to quake. Giufà has heard tell of these iron carts that run on four wheels without a horse or a mule to pull them, and make a din, and spit fire. He saw one once, on a fair-day, coming headlong down the zigzags at Biddini, an onslaught of flame and dust, and in it a head that was nothing but goggles and crowned with leather: who else but the Devil?

Much the same roaring and flashing he seems to hear and see now, as he puts his ear to the ground and squinnies through the undergrowth, though it's some time since he trusted those eyes, those ears. . . He who each spring, on his back in the fields, was once alive to the rustle of the growing grass, and with a stone, and from a distance, could hit a darting lizard. But the

41

days come and go, and your beard is white, and how you have changed, Giufà...

Giufà is alarmed at the dawn that is slow to break, and at night persisting, tumultuous and fierce. He drinks the three eggs, first caressing the liquid between the tongue and palate; but the way the ground shudders beneath the feet of machines in motion, the spurt of hot stench they belch out, traversing the hedge like the panting of a savage beast, and – between one and the next – the stupefied stillness of the countryside... it seems to Giufà, you see, that the whole wide world is sick, screaming in agony without relief. Worse than the earthquake a few years since, which was a thing of nature. But today it is men doing injury to themselves...

Giufà feels the stolen fowl fast cooling against his chest. To pluck and cook it he will need a knife, a scrap of dry tinder, two crossed rods for a spit. Accessories which the old man, muddle-headed as he is, knows where to find: in the abandoned roadman's hut right opposite, across the highway. He gets to his feet, sleepy, and makes towards it. He clambers through the hedge, plants his bare footsoles on the hard metalled surface. Only to stop dead, bewildered, blinded by two headlights that burst out round a bend, bear down on him. He knows he must flee, for a second he wants to, but he feels sought after, wanted, by those eyes. So he runs in the teeth of the foe, in the teeth of the Devil, arms flung wide (Stop, stop, Giufà! Where are you going? That iron contraption is not for you! Others have devised it to your ruin, to the ruin of your pastoral content-ment...). Without crossing himself he runs in the teeth of the Devil, with wrath and astonishment feels the four hoofs rear over him and crash down, shattering his bones and crushing, along with his ribs, his hidden booty of a stolen hen...

It was May 6th 1906, the day of the first Targa Florio motor race, but how was Giufà to know?

Trouser-peg's Revenge

THAT VINCENZO (i.e. Vincenzulu, i.e. 'Nzulu) Incardona, known as Trouser-peg, a weedy, ugly, penniless fellow, had married the superbly curvaceous Aida, was a fact. One might be incredulous, one might be scandalized, but the fact remained. Solid, indelible, furnished with every statutory civil and religious endorsement: the exchange of rings, the blessing of Father Giustino, a certificate from the mayor to exhibit on request to the most sceptical hotel receptionists both insular and peninsular. An unequal match if ever there was one, and equal only, perhaps, with that of Caesar and God. Like so many matches made in this world.

"'Nzulu," called Aida, leaning in at the doorway in all the pride of her womanhood, those 57 kilos of white, soft flesh, radiantly rosy here and there from that touch more blood suffusing it, and crowned with a ferocious forest of raven curls. He raised his eyes – myopic, adoring, shining with self-sacrifice and passion – from his coffee-cup. Thus it was that he had won her over, with this doglike look of inflexible servility. As if every instant he were offering her his soul, his entire life, on a charger. Ready to jump out of the window, no questions asked. And to kill, of course, were she but to whisper a name in his ear. Though it would have been a sight worth seeing, 'Nzulu Incardona with a pistol in his fist, he who was so awkward in his every movement of the day... He set off in the early hours with the mail-bag slung round his neck, on a bicycle without a chain-guard, instantly in need of someone to extricate his flapping trouser-bottoms from between chain and sprocket-wheel. Until he thought of pinning them with a clothes-peg, with the result that children used to give him chase, disrespectfully crying "Trouser-peg, Trouser-peg!". Indifferent, as children are, to the wince of distress that puckered his cheeks beneath the sweat and dust.

A positive disgrace, and an affront to the dignity of the Post Office, as office manager Sciveres was wont to bewail from out his cloud of smoke at the Club. This Sciveres, having transferred him for a week to the telegram guichet and received countless more complaints about 'Nzulu sedentary than 'Nzulu itinerant, had finally resolved to re-assign him, with the old uniform but a new bag, to his former duties.

So "'Nzulu," called Aida, and he raised his head, vowed obedience with his eyes, told her with his eyes, "I am here, I am yours, do with me what you will." And what she willed was not little, or at least not less than the usual, which was no small thing. This was for her to hunt through the pile of letters he brought home before starting his round and choose the two or three envelopes she considered most promising; and in the winking of an eye to steam them open, read them and reseal them. Just for fun and games, and the venomous pleasure of espionage. And also, at the thought of being able to see and to know unseen, to get a sensation so stunning as to keep her dazed for the rest of the day; as after a love-swoon, one of those into which she fell in his skinny arms every Saturday, when poetically closing her eyes in the dark and mentally transforming him into a manlier man, an actor, for example, recently adored on the silver screen at the Odeon: Nils Asther, Ronald Colman. . . Until the time when, strolling beneath the palm-trees in the Corso, she discovered a closer and more appetizing resemblance in the glad-eyes and mustachios of Nenè Bocchieri the municipal policeman.

"'Nzulu," called Aida yet again. This time the name rang

out an octave higher, demanding a further act of obedience, according to a ritual practised between them for months past. It meant he should get out and leave her alone with her peccadillo. "Because," she explained, "what the eye doesn't see the heart doesn't grieve over. You must see nothing. If they tumble to something you must be able to swear you know nothing, that you've seen nothing. And now take yourself off to the bathroom," she stormed, seeing her husband giving her a queer look as he sat with his coffee untouched before him. For 'Nzulu was somehow jealous of those emotions which excluded him, and would in his mild way have liked to share them, less to pry into secrets than out of an ingenuous need of connivance with her.

Yet this time also he obeyed submissively and left the room. Content that Aida would shortly be calling him again, and he would see the customary glow of pleasure and triumph in her eyes, the flush of scarlet on her cheeks, as after a stolen kiss. For 'Nzulu Incardona knew not what sort of trafficking was afoot to his injury and through his own agency. A smooth and simple dodge which Aida had invented and assiduously studied and brought to perfection, until it became an infallible mechanism. Briefly, the policeman would post his missives to his lady-love, addressing them to himself. She would substitute them in the same envelopes with impassioned replies of her own, salt with tears and peppered with laughter, lamentations and vows sworn in the name of the Deity. Leaving to 'Nzulu, poor fellow, the role of unsuspecting courier of love. No slight intended on her part, however; in fact, in her own way, Aida had never ceased to be fond of him. Like some object or garment grown old along with us, an alarm-clock, a sweater, that we don't throw away without a pang. . .

Ah, what a fiery epistle Aida had written the policeman this time! With what a fluttering and cooing of the heart did she reseal the envelope, while next door she heard the honest chain-pullings and throat-clearings and whistlings of *Rigoletto* that formed the refrains of 'Nzulu's ablutions. What flutterings

45

indeed! For this time she had decided to take the final step, and in her message she promised the man a tryst. Tomorrow, at her house, when her husband had left it, not to return from his round till the familiar midday Angelus.

As for 'Nzulu, Fate so decreed that, making a tight turn outside the San Giuseppe flour mill, he should skid on a surface sleek with recent rain and ride his velocipede smack into a wall of sacks. A bit of good luck – worse luck! He got to his feet unhurt, in fact, only slightly grazed at the knees and floury, but the mail-bag flew open at the impact and the letters flew out. What a boon – what a bombshell! For the hand of irony retrieved them from the puddle and Fate decreed that the muckiest and muddiest of all should be the letter sent by Nenè Bocchieri to Signor Bocchieri Nenè; and that 'Nzulu should think it proper to rectify matters by replacing the envelope with a new one, copying the address with his own hand; and that in the process there should fall from the first envelope a lock of hair of a colour which the postman knew in the core of his being; and that swift investigation should lay bare, not only in that love-token but in a well-known handwriting and Aida's shameless signature, proof of a betrayal that would have made the angels blush. . .

It is told (and here down south there's no truth but is myth and no myth but is truth) that 'Nzulu Incardona spent a whole hour pacing back and forth in the yard of the old mill, muttering and gesticulating to himself. That then, remounting his bicycle, he made his delivery from street to street in a singularly careful and leisurely fashion, and then returned home to assume docility and ignorance until the morrow. But that at dawn, setting forth to do his round, he concealed himself instead around the corner, waiting for the policeman to fall into the trap. And that, armed with planks, nails and a hammer, he then firmly sealed up the front door, resoundingly summoning all and sundry to come and get an eyeful of the imprisoned lovers, now at the window pleading for mercy. And that finally, laughing and crying together, crouched over his handlebars lower than any Fausto Coppi, he sped out of town, off, off past Mazzarrone, past Dirillo, all the way to the reservoir at Licodia, there to drop into the water like a stone, not without first shedding on the parapet one sad trouser-peg.

Ciaciò and the Puppets

THE CHARNEL-HOUSE of the paladins was in a corner of the loft of Donna Ignazia's house. Up there they lay in heaps, helmets skew-whiff like the caps of *mafiosi*, faces peeled down to the papier mâché, wooden skeletons peeping through rents in their skirts.

New to the place, Ciaciò put forward an exploratory foot, keeping the other in reserve, glued to the top step while he peered intently into the darkness. His candle was not much help; it took a beam of moonlight through a crack in the roof to disclose the bodies and faces in a jumble of acrobatic and tragic poses: the same scene, almost, as in the show earlier in the evening, set in the valley of Roncesvalles, only here it was not death-throes produced by jerking strings, but a passive catastrophe, inglorious and irremediable.

"I'm a puppet too," the boy commiserated with himself – and felt the back of his neck pricked by the metal hook of an invisible string.

He was distracted by a mouse emerging from a Saracen's turban, a fearless mouse furnished with grey whiskers, who stopped three handsbreadths short of his shoe and observed him at length with critical condescension. Better not to let him have his head, so Ciaciò resolved to enter, not without first sniffing the air to sample its quality.

It was good, perfumed with an aroma of melons so pungent as to swamp the whiff of mouse. So his dreams tonight would be melon-scented dreams. For, mice or no mice, it was here that he was going to have to sleep, while Mastro Rutilio was already snoring in Donna Ignazia's bed. . .

He cocked an ear: the rumble of that snoring rose through the dark like the roar of a wild beast. It wasn't proper that it should also come to the ears of Ninfa in her exile under the stairs. Donna Ignazia would have done better, for the nonce, to have sent her daughter into the country. . .

A scalding drip fell on his hand. It was time to settle down. He dripped more wax on the floor and stood the candle in it, then stretched out fully dressed on the horsehair mattress, pulling the blanket up to his chin. It wasn't the first time: he'd spent hundreds of nights like this since his orphanage days, surrounded by mice and strings of hanging melons, in lofts, barns, doss-houses, in every borough and parish in the county. . .

He looked over at the mouse which had followed these operations without stirring. "Rapscallion," he called him, softly spelling out the syllables, in memory of another mouse, a white ball of fluff, his companion for years in his days of fortune-telling from door to door, before he apprenticed himself to Rutilio the puppeteer.

"Rapscallion," he called again, gently, to strike up a conversation, but the mouse appeared not to hear him. He did a quick right-about turn and scampered off to hide beneath King Agramante's cloak.

Rutilio and Ignazia had known one another since childhood, when they were in service on the same estate. It was she, not yet thirteen years old, who had teased him and egged him on, darting out from every hedge, half dressed, half not, dusty, giggling, with those two quinces of flesh hardening on her chest and the stalk of a yellow flower between her teeth. Until he crashed down on top of her, "Mammamia, mammamia!", blindly convulsed with pleasure from head to foot without knowing what to do about it, while she, blindly as he, nevertheless unearthed gestures, words and gasps from some remote closet of instilled knowledge, bestowing her limbs appropriately beneath him in a duel and mingling and alleluia of the blood; nor afterwards would they remember how long it lasted or when it began and ended. All the same, from the morrow on, whenever they met they looked daggers at each other, began to avoid each other, almost to throw stones at each other from afar... Then Rutilio was called up, Ignazia married early. To meet again thirty years later, one midday, both of them widowed, he in Spaccaforno with his puppets and looking for a night's lodging. He had recognized her at the street door, acting the brisk housewife, but the sway of the hips and the lean brown limbs and the dark eyes were as of yore; so that even while still in the street, with no regard for her daughter, who was looking on, he had slipped a hand inside her dress...

Thenceforth he made a habit of dropping in at her place whenever he could, for a night or two, to recover from work, and the heat and the cold, and travelling from fairground to festival the length and breadth of the island; and to warehouse there his broken puppets, spare heads, discards. Up in that loft was a sort of depot behind the lines, an emporium along a caravan route. The women avidly awaited these stopovers. Not only Ignazia but her daughter Ninfa as well: growing up, she was, by leaps and bounds with each day that passed, artful in glance and in bearing, ever more resembling her mother, her lips parted, her nostrils always a-quiver to catch whatever male scent or step might come to her through the window.

Ciaciò turned over on his horsehair sack and rubbed a finger across both eyes. Supper had been on the heavy side: spaghetti with cuttlefish sauce and rabbit fried in breadcrumbs. And to finish up, a pudding dripping with chocolate, which seemed to melt in your mouth and take your tongue along with it, each mouthful refreshing the memory of its predecessor. Not to speak of the vintage wine – a strong, dark Cerasuolo – which Ciaciò felt still heavy in his limbs as he rolled over this way and that with the film-show of the evening playing back before his eyes: the two oldsters, gluttonous for food but even more for each other, playing footy-footy under the table, and Ninfa, excited enough herself, drinking like any grown-up and never tiring of "Where have you come from, where have you been, when are you going to Catania?"

Mastro Rutilio had then started to relate the new sketch he was preparing for his début in the big city, and shown them the poster with eight coloured squares representing the story of Lady Rovenza, of how she vowed to avenge the slaying of her brother Oldauro, and laid siege to Paris, and was invincible, every part of her person being enchanted except (the puppeteer had here lowered his voice, glancing furtively at Ninfa with belated qualms about upsetting her)... except the very seat of her womanhood, in the unattainable groin; and how Rinaldo shammed dead on the battlefield until she should pass her slain foes in review, and caught her in that place with a sudden upthrust, eliciting therefrom a great piss-drench of dark blood and death... At which Rutilio had started splitting his sides with uncontrollable laughter, while Ninfa lowered her eyes and Ignazia drummed her fists on his belly crying "What a buffoon you are, what a buffoon! Come on, it's late, let's get to bed."

In Ciaciò's mind, between waking and sleeping, all this was now creating pandemonium and restless dreams, interspersed with liberating draughts of air, which mingled with the delicate odour of melons a more vigorous tang of garlic, and to some extent lent warmth to the congealed chill of the attic.

With this comfort he was waiting upon morning when he heard his name called by a trumpet voice. He opened his eyes on night. A blur of half-light, like wan moonshine oozing through the cracks in the roof, was floating above his head. Tepid moon in tepid water, however. Even though it was mid-September and he had already felt the early sting of autumn, like the tiniest prick of a knife-point under the ribs.

Tepid moonlight, tepid water, and in it Ciaciò was swimming with listless strokes, so listless that they seemed to make no headway, to leave him in mid-air, in a tender, gentle eddy, undulant as one of his puppets, attached to a single string. Peace reigned now, all but a muted creaking, as of bare feet cautiously climbing wooden steps. A tenuous waft, a tentative breath. Or rather, perhaps, a sigh?

No time to figure this out, the trumpet had sounded his name again and he set out to follow it, speeding through endless corridors of clouds, his footsoles skimming the downy flocks, the spongy bunches of cirrus, brushing aside with one hand stars and thunderbolts. A whopping great God the Father flashed in and out of a sky-blue porthole, like the name of a station glimpsed through a train window. Ciaciò had scarcely registered his smile before the trumpet shrilled in his ears again, manifestly spurring him on to an appointment.

"What's all this?" he wondered, though vaguely hoping not to get an answer; for it was pleasing thus to slide, without encountering anything hard or bumpy, into a funnel of moist, mysterious contentment.

It didn't last. Now the ground had hardened beneath his feet, a woodland pathway firm to his feet through the drifts of fallen leaves. A wood suitable for hunting parties, for single combats, where the trumpet blared still louder, excruciating, more a summons to Judgement than a tantivy. And Ciaciò beheld, descending slowly slowly, and coming to rest in the centre of the clearing, gigantic, caparisoned in gold and silver and monarchically plumed, the horse that is called Hippogryph.

An animal? Was it simply an animal? For beneath the triumphant plume and storiated blinkers its nostrils drooped with almost human melancholy, while the swish of its tail against its flanks, and the striking of its hoofs on the ground, certainly intended in their way to express a thought.

Lawk-a-mercy, what to do? Ciaciò was at a loss. The horse seemed to be getting at him, to want to tell him something.

All the more clearly so when, fanning the air with his calm, majestic amble, he came and knelt down at his feet, plainly inviting him on his back as rider and master.

Lawks, what to do? The Hippogryph was more finely apparelled than a patron saint, all a glitter of polished studs and tinkle of bell-harness. A plume of red and green pheasant quills rose between his ears; an arabesqued saddlecloth cascaded from his back; and copper studs, stars, braids, embroideries, rosettes, and medallions, scattered everywhere, from noseband to girth, all but immersed his every limb. His mane, now that he was stooping, shook in leonine undulations, while his wings, though folded and limp like becalmed sails, trembled from time to time under the hand that caressed them, set a-quiver beneath the skin by an electric urge to flight.

Ciaciò knew not what to do: the temptation was great. He stroked the steed, he spoke to it, sensed it to be docile and eager. But he had scarcely slipped a foot into the stirrup before he was arrested by a cry for help from a dishevelled Angelica fleeing among the trees and pursued by a black-bannered infidel, the famous Gattamogliere.

"Christian knight!" cried the lovely damsel to Ciaciò. "Have pity on me, a star-crossed Christian maid of very gentle lineage!"

And so saying she fell at his feet, even as the Moor stormed up. Ciaciò awaited him unflinching, his tongue already itching with a tirade he knew by heart, one of Rinaldo's he had heard countless times intoned by Mastro Rutilio while he was steadying the stool under him or oiling the pulleys in the wings of the booth. He'd recited it under his breath often enough, those June–July evenings, each time the puppet-master unhitched the mules and took a nap under the cart after a blowout of bread and sardines. Ciaciò, for his part, preferred to sit in the midst of his puppet family, cleaning them up, conversing with them, begging them for a story: in vain unless, acting out all the parts in turn, he made himself up one...

"Gattamogliere," he declaimed accordingly, wielding a

branch picked up from the ground. "Mighty indeed are you against women, but it behoves you more, in my belief, to do combat with a man!" And to the girl: "Fear not, gentle maiden, for were there a hundred of them as he is one, they would not harm one hair of your golden tresses." But Gattamogliere laughed: "This fellow is courting death." Then, advancing on him: "How do you dare, base churl, to cross my path?"

Ciaciò put up his guard, and in the wood the silence grew immense. The Hippogryph, which seemed disposed for sleep, delegating to a lazy ripple of muscles the task of keeping the flies at bay, suddenly reared its tail as straight as a sapling and pawed determinedly with one hoof at the trunk of a carob. In the midst of its coils a snake opened an eye, on the lofty gallery of a top branch perched a bird.

"Commend your soul to your Mahound," quoth Ciaciò, settling his rustic lance into its rest and planting himself, legs astraddle, in the centre of the pathway. But the other was already upon him in buoyant jousting style, as when on feast days they tilt at a quintain, and watching from the dais is the king's daughter.

Naught did it avail him: with a crafty caper the boy eluded the lance and his weapon-point was quick to find his opponent's windpipe, where a slim lace collar left the flesh exposed between chin and gorget. Though not without the Moor, on the instant of giving up the ghost through his gullet, stinging his cheek with a counterstroke. Both fall to the ground, the dead and the wounded man, but over the latter lo! already the damsel is lovingly bending; she raises him in her arms, floods him with the deluge of her golden tresses, draws on his wound with her lips, not removing them even when the languished warrior manifests, with quickened breath and rekindled visage, the verve and fervour of recovered health. . .

Ciaciò came to. A flesh-and-blood girl was curled up beside him under the blanket, the sheen of a moonbeam on her brow. "Will you let me sleep beside you?" whispered the voice of Ninfa. In her white nightdress with its red Greek-fret border which made her look like a girl in boarding-school, she had crept in quiet as a mouse and curled up at his side. Heaven knows how long she had been there looking at him without a word.

Ciaciò was much startled. The flood of moonlight revealed a small face framed by two thick plaited tresses resting on the shoulders, from which sprang two bare, fledgling arms. But the voice was a woman's, hoarse and throaty, reminding him of the turkeys pecking around the marquis of Scordia's yard in his boyhood days.

"Ninfa! What on earth are you doing here?" was the most he could think of saying, while with his palms he made as if to parry her words and keep them from the distant ears of Rutilio and Donna Ignazia. So he shifted closer to her, speaking with his lips right in her hair, in a whisper that was already half a kiss. She, as far as possible in the tiny space between his body and the wall, eluded him, fugitive and shy, but none the less submissive. "I'm cold," she said, "but you're not to lay a finger on me. I only want to stay here in the warm, away from *them*." A touch of rancour warped her voice. She couldn't altogether like Rutilio's intrusion into the family, even though at each visit she seemed on top of the world. Maybe she was a mite jealous of her mother...

Such were the lad's thoughts, though higgledy-piggledy as his notions always were, stirred but lightly by a frisson of sensuality, a throb of physical exhilaration that ousted clear thinking but which now was itself supplanted by one overriding anxiety: lest the girl's audacity were discovered, and he lost his apprenticeship, and was forced back to his old starvation and vagrancy, now in the lock-up now out under the stars, a gypsy life all trouble and no trade, always a slave to need, if not worse masters still.

"Go away!" he begged her with his hands; but she was unperturbed. On the contrary, "Be good. Go to sleep," she told him in such a commanding tone that Ciaciò shut his eyes again, touching only an elbow against her chest to learn the warmth of it, then falling back instantly into the same dream as before: same time, same place, no more and no less. As happens to innocent minds that walk the shifting watershed of time, and readily muddle up lying fables with true ones.

So here he is, back in the wood and in the arms of the hunted maiden, while the sun comes and goes among the leaves, mimicking the flash of gold Napoleons in a hand snapping open and shut. The Hippogryph has made no movement: it might be a dragon on guard over the corpse of Gattamogliere. But the stillness is short-lived, broken by the persistent *cracracrah* of enraged cicadas.

Ciaciò lets the music take him, rock him from branch to branch in a rise and fall of waves ever more subdued, as when the wind drops and the undertow leaves barely a stipple of froth among the rocks, the dwindling caresses of a manifold hand...

So then... is this what they call love? Two people together, their two breaths mingled into one, which is the selfsame vagabond breath of the sea? And this tremor, this honeyed death and rebirth and dying again of all the roots of the heart, this cooing of voices and tongues in the dishevelment of tresses...

Or is love another and a harder thing: a blind sword-stroke, Rinaldo's blackguardly thrust at Donna Rovenza?

Ciaciò in his sleep tensed himself to understand it, but the damsel had already forsaken him and approached the recumbent beast. Suddenly she mounted it, without a backward glance. The Hippogryph snapped open its wings: it had been waiting for nothing else. Ciaciò saw it splay out in the air like an enormous fan – he was forced to duck his head at the gust of its passing. He had scarcely time to glimpse, from below, the four hoofs prancing among the treetops, sparkling in the sunlight, before the great bird was a mere speck high overhead, which a cloud gathered up and obliterated.

*   *   *

When Ciaciò's eyes reopened Ninfa had gone. He was alone with the puppets in their corner, a platoon of wan, misshapen spectres. Among them Astolfo, one-armed and plumeless; Orlando, squint-eyed, bandy-legged; Gano, hacked in three pieces... Oh Gano, if you aren't the image of Mastro Rutilio – the same moustaches, the same expression! But you too, Fioravante, you too Rizieri, you too Guerino the Luckless – how you have fallen from your thrones of valour! What sort of warriors are you now, no wars, no worth...

Ciaciò was reminded of the ossuary he had once seen in the Cappuchin church in Còmiso, where the holy fathers and hermits lay stretched in their homespun habits, but turned to bone-dust, cinereous sentinels of nothingness. Thus comes an end to parlance and to prowess. Thus, once, to the Paladins of France, and thus, tomorrow, to Ninfa and Ciaciò. And Ninfa, where had she gone? Had she ever come up here at all? The boy searched the mattress for a warm hollow, a hair, any sign whatever. Nothing did he find; the air still smelt of sweet melon and of mouse. He licked his lips to distinguish the saliva of another, but found only the sour aftertaste of last night's feast. His head was aching now, it felt like lead, unsteadily affixed to the slender stem of his neck. "I'm a puppet too, worse off than them," he thought again, giving a last look to the troop of scattered, shattered figures. Then he climbed down from the loft and groped in the meagre light of dawn towards the summoning voice. Mastro Rutilio was already washed and dressed: they had to be off. Another day's life to be lived.

After the Flood
OR
The Rude Awakening

THROUGH THE SLIT in the planking the light at water-level had a dismal look, a viscous mish-mash almost thick enough to touch, had it not broken and dispersed at the mere probe of the eye. Light?... But what sort of light is a light nor of sun nor of moon, but a mere oleagenous olive-green evanescence, an undulous oily air clotted round the hull? It was tempting to strike it with an oar, puncture it with a harpoon; a hostile thing, among the countless vapours that rose from the whirlpools, hovered an instant above them – then seen no more. And swarthy tree-trunks, fleets of bodies drowned and swollen, tatters of black miasma trapped between waves, ominous mirages...

Noah was sick and tired of keeping his eyes peeled day and night at one side window or the other as if through a second set of eyelids, sick of having always to peer from his lookout seat at the same slab of catastrophe, never letting his attention wander to the pandemonium of the human and animal voices roaring behind his back...

With this he had wanted no truck from the start, loath as he was to mix with that fearful rabble, even with those closest to him, his own flesh and blood, let alone with the more alien creatures. Let them eat, sleep and copulate to their hearts' content down in the bowels of the ark. He himself had squatted in this lookout nook with no company but the bowls where each morning his wife silently deposited his ration of food and drink. Here he had camped and kept watch, scoring a notch in the wood with a nail for every day of flood foretold by the Voice. When that night was over the notches would number one hundred and fifty.

Although there was no earthly way of steering her in such a predicament, the vessel was finely built and Noah was modestly proud of her. As nimble as she was robust, pitch-painted within and without, in length three hundred cubits, in breadth fifty cubits, in height thirty cubits. . . And, hurricane-lashed, she gave off such an aroma of resin as to stiffen the sinews of the heart. It was enough for Noah, when the weather was at its foulest, and the winds howled strongest, and the end seemed nearest, to stretch out directly over the keel, with only the thickness of the planking between his body and the abyss; it was enough to inhale a great lungful of that odour of wood, the odour of uplands and of forests, of still-quick life, homely and innocent, and his heart was gladdened. A house and a home was the ark, scudding over the waters of darkness, as careless and unsinkable as a bird's feather.

Much more than any feather in truth, to him as captain. More like a floating mountain spur, a many-storeyed fortress, with its cross-beamed roof and door caulked with a double layer of pitch. The ark! After so many days the man almost loved it. And to make himself all the more master of it he had fashioned a rope ladder with which to climb from deck to deck, brisk despite his years (which were innumerable) and forever on the go, up and down, here at a peephole to scan the waters – how they roared and rolled, turbid and hostile – or there on the highest eyrie, lashed to a spar, to spy out some hint of remission on the horizon. And never, never, as far as the eye could see, glimpsing anything but a looming and crashing avalanche of leaden cataracts, blind walls that at the eleventh hour opened before the gopher-wood cockle, only to lay hold on it again, toss it back playfully, while he kept watch in his cubbyhole, oddly content to live in the eye of that liquid fury as once, before debouching into life, in the lake of his mother's womb.

Between this man and that body of water, that beast without end, for one hundred and fifty days there had reigned a momentous state of war. Not even a truce on the morrow? He knew not what answer to give himself, though every so often, less as a sop than a scoff, he would snatch up some morsel at random to hurl into the enemy's mouth, and liked to watch it dance for an instant round a whirlpool before it sank and vanished.

He listened: a riot of voices reached him from some invisible spot at his back. Sure to be his three sons rolling dice as usual, before the inevitable wifely audience. While the rest of the "crew", beasts both pure and impure, each couple cramped into its slip of a cell, lay immersed in the obtuse indolence of total thraldom. So be it. He could cope on his own with what small manoeuvres were possible, as he had all these months, marking up the days and nights, in the absence of heavenly bodies, according to the alternations of sleep and waking, to which his members were fortunately still obedient.

A memento of living, a guarantee of living again, was this loyalty of his body to the venerable armistice of sleep... And not without dreams: dreams, wafted by music, of tranquil hours hard by a coppice-side... dreams of the earth, of seasons and stars, as they might perchance be remembered after death. Of the earth as once it was, its ears of wheat and clusters of grapes, its breezes and lithesomeness of running waters struck of a sudden by a sparkle of sunlight. Dreams that were kindled glimmerings, firefly-glimmerings kindled in the darkness of a sole terrestrial memory, alone on a shuddering deck at the mercy of ocean; one memory, one only, throbbing on an unpeopled globe and posting across the fields of eternal silence whence the Voice first reached his ears...

He scanned the sky for a point known only to him, but above

his head discerned only a cavern of dark, the fissure of a weeping eye whence the flood appeared to teem, like an unbounded spate of tears. It was He, Jehovah in person, whose single slit of an eye was weeping thus, and his lamentations were nimbus and night, tumult and death. Would they ever be appeased, that wrath and that sorrow? And would it ever speak again, that Voice? The Voice, inaudible to others, which Noah believed he heard one morning, and heard in it the pledging of an oath, a covenant, a pact of love... And of salvation, resurrection, life...

For the hundred and fiftieth time he plunged the lead into the deep, knowing full well that it was idle to think of measuring the waters. For this he chose the rare intervals between two storms, when the most obstreperous inclemencies gave place to mere rain, that icy, immutable, plumbeous, pelting rain... On these occasions, if the vessel chanced to be once more rocking in the vicinity of some submerged massif, whose peaks might be glimpsed below the billows, and whose rocky barrier had in the first days provided a reef-encircled refuge; if, I say, the vessel was about to approach a depth within reach of the anchor-chain, the old man cast his sounding-line into the deep, heedless of endangering the keel against some hidden peak. Thus it was now: he heard a joist grind under his feet, saw a dribble of murky brine seep in through a seam and snake its way across the boards. Nor was the man dismayed, but almost joyful. For that unseen obstacle meant firm ground not far below, meant that some fragment of the earth's surface he had indeed touched, even if his sons had taken a knock...

It was his first re-encounter with terra firma since, from the ark, he had seen the topmost pinnacles of a city crumble, incinerated by a thunderbolt, sizzling like forge-irons plunged into water. He was therefore almost joyful, and tore the clothes off his back, fashioned them into a bung to fill the crack, sealed it with expert hands. Then he clambered to the roof and three times over shouted his name at the waters.

*   *   *

61

The hundred and fifty-first day: Noah rose early. It was still raining, in scattered showers. The sky was still black, though with a blackness ripe for repentance. The ocean too seemed eager to change its skin, its colour altered at each new gust of wind; and these were smooth, vehement and magnanimous, the vigorous sighs and breaths of God. It seemed to the Patriarch that he heard words in that wind, but knew not what they meant; had it not been that, on reaching out from his poky-hole with upturned palms, he drew them in again as dry as before. He passed them across his face, and they were dry.

He had no wish to call his sons, he said not a word to his wife, but huddled in his nook to recogitate a thought that had already once filled his mind, uncertain whether it was one of joy or of terror, an amorphous thought within which he fell asleep. When he awoke, and had climbed to the roof of the ark, even in that brief time small eminences had laboured their way into the light, and rose streaming from the universal ruin. On this side two crests rose to create a channel, beyond fanned out a delta, elsewhere the choppy waters proclaimed a shallows. The vessel itself, albeit so black and pitchy, resembled a swan that glides from bank to bank, and with its wings rejoiceth.

Whereupon, like the collapse of a sail, of a pavilion, the roof of cloud went limp, arrows of light fragmented it, a gigantic seven-hued bow arched on the instant across the sky. And a round red sun, beside itself with joy, beamed upon the world as on an immensurable copper shield. The man whistled the dove to his shoulder, and thence with a whisper sent it forth towards the things of this earth.

One morning Noah decided to emerge. The dove had returned, departed, returned once more and departed again. He no longer expected it back, and his heart was aglow. Out he went, the sprig of olive in his hand, with bare foot cautiously probing the blanket of yellow mud in which the vessel had settled.

His first steps were those of a drunkard. But he pressed stoutly on, floundering knee deep, scaling a ridge that promised a panorama. Step by step he gained the height, from a shelf of rock looked out at last, with eyes avid to baptize and cherish the virgin earth. He looked, and he loved it: befouled with stains and mildews, smoking with volcanos, pitted with a thousand pools, but glittering, O how glittering, with rejoicing and youth!

On his way back down his eye was caught by a triangle of flood-water trapped in a rocky hollow. He was not displeased by the face reflected in it, seared by wind and salt, furrowed by a thousand alarms. A face majestic with years, but new-fledged withal and lost in wonder, as was the world; and sparkling like the earth with a subterranean smile. Which burst into a bellow of laughter on his hearing the uproar at the door of the ark, from which, free of all bonds, the families – pedestrian, volatile, reptilian – now swarmed out running, crawling or winging their way to caves or nests or lairs. His own three sons, Shem, Ham and Japhet, he saw setting out, each on his own road. Only the woman was silent, at his side; and he stroked her hair with his hand.

"Behold!" he said, with a sweep of his arm that embraced the earth, the archipelagos, the gulfs, the crystal of the air, the meanderings of valleys and of rivers, the amphitheatre of the horizons. A sweetish stench of decay still rose from it, but already from the slime burgeoned mysterious seeds, diamond droplets trembled on the fronds, aerial roots stretched forth to drink of them, the eyes of small creatures glittered lively in the grass.

The old man raised his eyes to the sky, expectant. Immensely blue and empty, the sky was, but for a quizzical rainbow paling there. Then on high appeared a dove, his dove, and seemed to sideslip on clumsy wings, dazzled by the sun. Noah did not spy the hawk, he did but hear a fluttering, a squawk, the thud of a white blur at his feet, which spattered his legs with blood from its torn throat.

63

But why?... Noah pricked up his ears in apprehension, narrowed suspicious eyes at the world. Dumbstruck, mistrustful, he took stock of the new-delivered earth. And he heard the wrathful voices of his sons, he saw a fist close round a stone, a spider spin a web between two stems, while nearby buzzed a fly. A wolf went howling after a lamb, a viper sank its fangs into a heel... *But why?* This the man asked the woman with his eyes, and with her eyes the woman gave him answer. A tear slid down Noah's cheek, trickled into his beard. He wiped it away with the back of his hand, and with humped shoulders, muttering, went his way:

"But Why? But Why?"

The Builder of Babel

I SAW HIM EVERY DAY when I went to the bar for my nine o'clock coffee, and found him still there in the evening, sitting at the same marble table with a bagful of books beside him and a biro at action stations between his index and middle fingers. Bald, squat, wild-eyed, and shot through every five minutes by a tic that sent several volts through his face. A feverish reader, he broke off every so often to jot down a phrase on a notepad, then read on. An anonymous client, they told me in the bar, but they called him Crusoe.

One morning I found out why. It had started to rain, and I was compelled to linger. Bored with being sole spectator to two pensioners playing the pinball machine, I sat down opposite him and introduced myself. He did not reciprocate, but pointed to the title of an article in an illustrated magazine hot off the press: *Back to Methuselah*, and its subtitle: *Human Lifespan Longer*. And as I showed signs of approval, eyeing me with mingled indignation and forbearance he delivered himself thus:

"Longer, eh? So what! Good luck to the lot of 'em. But the real advantage would be if, vice versa, the universe of knowledge were to be reduced. What use is this longevity, when into the valise of your skull you will have failed to cram so much as a thousand millionth part of what is knowable? Time was when it sufficed to live forty years and study Pliny's *Natural History* to be able to die in peace, replete with vistas and visions. But today so many are the books, the theatres, the pictures, the musical compositions, the faces, scenes and skies of far-off lands, and so meagre is the part of them which falls to each one of us, as to discourage all intellection, all thirst for knowledge. . ."

I was not forearmed for a weighty discussion. "Why not rest content with that little," I suggested. "With the little our eyes and our years bestow on us. Lots of people are perfectly happy with it."

He flew into a rage. "Happy! How can they be if in Lincolnshire there is a *Salomè* by Guido Reni they'll never see, if they'll never read Cardan's *Ars Magna*, never kiss the lips of Clorinda down there at the cash desk? How can we be happy if we can have so little of the all or the muchness that we crave?"

So petulantly did he speak that Clorinda from a distance heard her name being bandied, and to be on the safe side smiled the most vermillion of her smiles. "The third impossibility," quipped I, "seems to me not wholly impossible. . ."

"You only half grasp the point," he reproached me, switching with patronizing rudeness to the familiar form of address. "For every available girl behind a cash desk there remain millions of unavailable ones in all four corners of the earth. If only for lack of time, of energy, of chances to meet. The same thing with books: even if we die very old we will still die over-young and empty-handed."

I gave him rope: "As regards today, I concede your point. But what about the future?"

"Worse," he replied firmly. "In a hundred thousand years, when by dint of vitamins and transplants man will have come to usurp the long life of the Patriarchs of old, he will find himself buried by such a mass of paper that he will be able to consume it only in pharmaceutical doses. One line for Napoleon – no more! – and one for Hitler, if they are to make room for all their numerous colleagues whom history has seen fit to spawn in the meantime. For one thing is unquestionable: in a hundred thousand years world affairs will invariably be expounded to the students of the time in a three-volume textbook, at an average of three hundred and thirty-three point three recurring centuries per volume: a page per century, in fact."

This had never occurred to me, and the prospect tickled me. "Our poor politicians!" I wailed. "The entire twentieth century in barely thirty lines by sixty spaces! They'll be jam-packed, I'm afraid. As for present-day writers and their chances of survival. . ."

He murmured then, suddenly bashful, "I think I might have a remedy. No!" he corrected himself. "What am I saying, remedy! A paltry prosthesis, but at all events better than nothing. I refer to Robinson Crusoe's desert-island book."

I gave him an enquiring look. He regained his self-confidence, waxed didactic: "Tell me, what books do you think Crusoe will take to his island next time? Or rather, since his baggage will presumably be pocket-sized, what single book?"

I was about to open my mouth, but he silenced me with a hand: "The Bible, the *Mahabharata*, *Das Kapital* as told to the proletariat? Not a bit of it! No, it will be the most up-to-date edition of a Dictionary of Quotations: "*Dispar et Unum*", "The Apple Eve Ate", "The Ultimate ABC", or whatever the hell they'll call it. . ."

"A miscellany of bons mots," said I, dubiously.

"A miscellany, yes," he cut in. "No other vade-mecum or 'black box' is available to one desirous of safeguarding for our descendants in post-history at least a relict of what man has thought in his muddled way over the centuries."

"Is that all there is to it?" I asked. "A choice selection of potsherds wrapped in tinfoil? It doesn't strike me as such a great idea. Reminds me of that governor of Arizona or Nevada not long ago, who had a concentrated essence of our twentieth-century way of life sealed up in a specially-built concrete catacomb for the survivors of the next apocalypse. Is that the sort of thing you have in mind?"

"What of it?" he shrilled. "Not one of the tropes of rhetoric can hold a candle to your synecdoche, the small part standing for the whole; not one possesses such power of allusion and illusion. No wonder it is employed indiscriminately both for the sublimities of the Eucharist and the banal prescriptions of homeopathic medicine. Not forgetting the pious custom of the Ancients of enclosing with the buried man, as a funerary viaticum and epitome of his life, grains of corn, combs of bone, jewellery. . ."

"Our case is different," I objected. "It's a question of squeezing, pulping, mincing, reducing thousands and thousands of sublime pages and dishing up an indigestible stew of them. I prefer silence to such a prattling confab of eunuchs."

After a moment's pause, crumbling a lump of sugar in his saucer: "Meanwhile tomorrow or the next day comes the flood. . ."

"Storm in a teacup, like this morning's." And I silenced him by pointing through the window at the cloudless sky and pedestrians passing dry-shod to and fro.

With this I left him. I had an appointment.

He had aroused my curiosity. Asking here and there, I learnt that he had been librarian in a big city, but was given the sack over some obscure business to do with certain volumes – some said stolen, others said randomly mutilated with scissors. This second version was perhaps nearer the truth, seeing that one morning I came upon him scissors in hand, in the act of snipping at pages for sometimes minuscule scraps, joining them together with sticky tape and slipping them, between two layers of cellophane, into one of those folio albums in which architects keep their projects. I soon realized that his too was in a sense a building project, that of the builder of Babel, and inspired by a logic which, though for six days it had seemed to me perverse, on the seventh ended by winning me over.

This was when he allowed me to examine a few specimens of his work. An astounding enterprise, I saw at once, not to be compared with the run-of-the-mill collections of aphorisms which with strings of stale plagiarisms pillage one another for the same witty fibs; but rather – assembled by dint of readings as eccentric as you will – an epitome, positively Carthusian in its strictness, of memorable *incipit* and *desinit*, a *panopticon* and bric-à-brac and scrapbook and *merzbild* and digest and mine and mosaic and *summa* of maxims, epigraphs, insights, precepts, *greguerias, agudezas, obiter dicta, disparates, poisons, fusées,* open-Sesames, golden verses, Sibyl's leaves... a collage of countless splinters astutely pilfered from subterranean Postumias and stately Parthenons, to be offered to our impotence in exchange for the usual antiquated, unconsummatable nuptials with the dust and ashes of the past.

My first feeling was that of being of a Sunday on the beach at Ostia, but at once through the crush and uproar I glimpsed a design, that of summoning to testify on one and the same subject, be it grave or frivolous, the most dissonant and incongruous voices, from Job to Karl Kraus, from Nostradamus to Paul de Kock; from which resulted a quick-fire debate of ghosts at a table far from round, a mixture of Jacobin assembly and begowned academical assizes, in which *lachrymae rerum,* insults, pleadings, deathless syllables and ephemeral word-plays chased each other from end to end, flew back and forth like an exchange of volleys in a staggering intellectual and fantastical battledore and shuttlecock.

Imagine the heroic obtusity and long-suffering of Bouvard and Pécuchet at the service of a Montaigne, of a St Jerome. Imagine Faust, feeling crushed by the weight of a hundred bookshelves beetling above him, obtaining from Mephistopheles (at the price of his soul) the power to distil into a single tome the quintessence and the mystery, the truth and the beauty, of every written work: the Book of Books, the lone alembic that turns to solid gold the inexhaustible cascades of ink that have thundered into this world since someone wrote with a finger on the sand the very first word of terror or of love...

This was, albeit in skeleton, the work which lay before me on the marble table, and which I leafed through beneath the burning stare of Crusoe and the sardonic brow-knitting of the barman.

"The self is odious," proclaimed one paper slip, but others immediately and volubly retorted: "The statement of an envious Jansenist", "The most senile thing ever thought about mankind", "Your self may be odious but mine isn't. Mine I would love even in someone else. Do I have to act difficult just because it's mine?". . . And so on for quite a while, with Pascal, D'Aurevilly, Nietzsche, Gide, all squabbling like so many hens. . . While on another sheet Kafka tugged Baudelaire by the sleeve: "The Creation is not the Fall of God. We are just one of his bad moods, an off-day". . . Can you wonder if under the head-word "Moon" I heard, or thought I heard, the blue-notes of "Blue Moon" rise muted to the lips of Leopardi's Wandering Shepherd in Asia?

Crusoe went mad five weeks later. Suddenly, like a man struck down by an embolism. He came to the bar, by now our study during the slack hours between then and midday, and emptied his satchel on to the table: a bundle of jottings, the fruit of his spoils of the day before. I was surprised by the air of triumphant and fiendish conceit with which he set about the ritual reading. I realized immediately that these were apocryphal, quotations from non-existent works, constructed with such markedly derisory relish as to exclude them from any but undergraduate or frivolous use. I listened, however, smiled and applauded, convinced that he had merely decided to take a holiday. Except that he in all seriousness required them to be included in the Opus; nor would he admit that they were spurious, maintaining them to be discoveries of his own, from choice works nowhere to be found and unknown to the science of bibliography. For the sake of a quiet life I yielded, but I was uneasy, unable to imagine what he was hatching beneath such freakishness. I read and re-read the new contributions and fretted not a little. "Preferring a nourishing hemlock to my wife's coffee. . .": this, he claimed, was gleaned from a lost chapter of the *Memorabilia* of Socrates. There followed (from the *History of the Automobile* by Tristan Tzara and Isotta Fraschini) a pun on Lux and Fiat that took my breath away. And again, a native recipe from *Happy Tropics*, by Man Friday, deploring the inedibility of castaway-meat as "too tough for words". . .

Anxious to play along, when he turned to me I sank a fingertip into his cheek and said, "You're chubbier than ever, friend Crusoe. Have you gobbled up Man Friday yourself, by any chance?"

He took me by the arm and whispered darkly that he had.

From then on not a day passed without his bringing dozens of similar inanities, all transcribed on to narrow strips and glued to the large sheets I mentioned. No longer claiming to have disinterred them from some secret archive but to have dreamt them at daybreak, which is the hallmark of truth. "Oliphant solos, telegrams of few words!" he recited from an improbable *Chanson de Roland Barthes*. Or else tried to fob me off with the opening of a *Memoirs of a Bathing-Attendant* by one Phlebas the Phoenician: "Moses and Boudu were easy jobs, but for Narcissus I didn't quite make it. . ."

It occurred to me at this point that, if even the titles, authors and texts of his limitless peculium were by now hopelessly embroiled in his brain, like a jigsaw or a Meccano set gone bonkers, then an aspiration far from blind was directing his manoeuvres, some Esperanto was aiding the tongues of the labourers in his Babel. This last extravagance, for example, where characters from myth, poetry and the cinema splashed together in amniotic fluids, may well have been born of the resolve – in accord with a cheese-paring procedure which is one with the loftiest creation – to concentrate the greatest number of messages in the smallest possible space, as in the bridge player's bid "one club".

All the same, the day he sang me, *sotto voce*, an extract from *Les liaisons dangereuses* by Bixio and Cherubini, I felt obliged to break off our association.

I saw him again months later, one morning when it was teeming with rain, like the day of our first meeting. I was sheltering in a doorway in Via del Corso when he passed right by me. He seemed not to recognize me; he was talking to himself and proffering himself insouciantly to the streams cascading from the gutters. Protruding from one pocket of his ancient overcoat – and I had the clinical eye to recognize it at a glance – was a tattered notepad of the usual rubbish, the frail paper raft on which he was once more making ready to face the Flood.

"Crusoe!" I called, emerging from my refuge, but he didn't hear me. He went on his way, hatless, brolly-less, deaf to the motor-horns screaming in his face. I saw him shoot into the air and remain there longer than one would have thought possible, before crashing down on to the bonnet of a car.

"What's it called in Spanish?" I asked myself nonsensically instead of hastening to help him. I was thinking of that dummy of Goya's in the Prado, being tossed in a blanket by three girls, but I had no time to remember that it was *El pelele* before I saw him hop to his feet like a gymnast, brush down his clothes and set off again through the criss-cross frenzy of the traffic, stamping imperious feet and splashing mud right, left and centre from the puddles.

The Visions of Basil

OR

The Battle of the Wordworms and the Heroes

AND SO THE SENATE of the World – that is, the body which thus pompously styled itself – decided in a sudden access of zeal to defend from the epidemic at least the most noble of writings, and to preserve them in safety within a single fortress. Their choice fell on Mount Athos, a place unique, impregnable from the sea and with but few and impracticable approaches along its landward confines. Hither, from the archives and libraries of every nation, on a vessel thoroughly pitched and disinfected in advance, were brought the works which in the opinion of the savants deserved to survive and to conquer time. Pile upon pile of volumes, nor could they presume to protect all these in equal measure. But rather, the majority being distributed among the lesser monasteries, the remaining five-score, the most precious, were housed in a tower in St Gregory's, entrusted to the custody of the patriarch Spyris and his community, waiting until the men of chemistry should discover an antidote to the invincible Worm.

This latter was a variety of *trogium pulsatorium* which appeared in the West immediately after the Second Hecatomb, spreading everywhere with such rapidity as to suggest that a misanthropic Nature, frustrated in her design for extinguishing mankind by his own hand, had contented herself with at least

73

laboratories, this entirely new enemy, innocuous to the health of his body but deadly to his written monuments.

It was during the penultimate decade of the twenty-first century, an age of sated passions in which the recent plethora of death had produced an unhoped-for concord and community spirit among the scant millions of living men. Men whose blood, having by inurement survived the invisible *tabes* of the atom, was not thereby rendered the less fatigued and pallid. They were to be seen wandering like sleepwalkers, dropping at every street-corner and thereafter regaining their feet with effort; nor were they always clear in mind, or lucid in their discrimination between the true and the false.

Little wonder, then, that the novice Basil, appointed by Spyris to be guardian of the treasure, and immured along with it, became in his cloistered life neglected, left without any further instructions and no less a hostage than a gaoler to his troop of wraiths. Nor was it long before he found himself in the grip of a baneful sloth, such as in the course of sieges accompany the hours preceding the assault, and fell into a state of visionary languor.

He had, with the aid of his confrères Macarius and Nicephorus, already enclosed each tome in an impermeable plastic envelope, replaced the oaken shelves with others of more expedient metal, seen to it that prophylactic sulphurs should burn day and night on every threshold... With what result? That as soon as his two companions had returned to the duties of community life, he being coerced into a sentry-like solitude and reduced to seeing nought in the course of the twenty-four hours but a hand through a hatch delivering his dinner-bowl, the monk began to suffer this leisure-time as a positive excommunication, and to feel himself pricked beneath the skin by the former torments of the flesh.

This Basil was sturdy-limbed, of olive complexion, with a thick dark beard which all but concealed the wine-coloured birthmark across his cheek, that now and then, in the midday heat, appeared to glow like a brand in the thicket on his chin. At such times he was compelled to rush and plunge his head in a bucket until he felt all but at death's door, and thereafter, dripping and bristly, to throw himself on his knees in prayer: in that endless shuttling of days and nights a surviving resource, from which he emerged worn out as from some profligacy of love. Only to succumb at once to another and more unlawful recourse, that of daydreaming. . .

But morning was the hour of innocence, for it was inspection time, when with light touch he removed the envelopes from the shelves, scrutinizing them one by one with a strong lens to ascertain their state of health. He smoothed the transparent coverings with his fingers, viewed them against the light. The seals appeared intact, no breach had been opened by the Grub. Yet, faced with so many forbidden pleasures, he was each time visited by a forlorn enticement to sample a few of them, especially the ancient romances, by the light of a muffled lamp and in violation of the terms of his trust. One day at last he yielded, confident of the external defences and the immaculacy of his own person, convinced that such an infringement presented no dangers and that a thorough fumigation after each reading would suffice to keep the epidemic at bay. Thenceforward life was not such a hardship to him; it even became a pleasure. He read, he daydreamed, he prayed. Often all three at once. In this wise passed the autumn and the winter.

March brought the twittering of swallows to the bastions of the tower and a thunderous Aegean spray dashing joyfully on the rocks below. It was the first time for many years that the seasons appeared to submit to the rules and regulations of former times. To Basil those black flashes in the sky, that seething whiteness down below, as he beheld them from the window, meant an intimation, perhaps even an announcement, of rebirth. And soon good tidings arrived from the Capital of the World and he learnt of it through the hatch: the pestilence was coming to an end. He was sorry to hear this, for he had grown attached to the chimeras of his reading-desk. To Spyris, who urged him to discontinue the state of quarantine, he opposed the pretexts of caution, and requested an extension which the indulgent Patriarch did not have the heart to refuse. So the novice was left once more, and for a long time, in his own company.

Then it was that his visions began. Visions, not dreams. For his were leaden slumbers, and on waking he had no remembrance whatever of the semblances which must none the less have trespassed upon his mind, since oftentimes from neighbouring cells he was heard wailing and tossing by night upon his pallet... Visions; or rather, on the wall, affrays in shadow-pantomime, upon the tremulous hosts of which – whether it be that too much reading fermented in him some creative neurasthenia, or that it was due, after so long a silence, to a need for play-acting – he bestowed speech, the ability to laugh and to groan, and names. The names he gave were those of the heroes of his readings: a bloodless army of zombies, but for all that determined to stand firm. And they were there to a man. All those, I mean, who in the pages so feverishly and illicitly scanned had ever borne arms or donned shining armour. Their gravity was that of solemn veterans, drawn up to face the horde of Wordworms in the defiles of a Thermopylae. This was, in fact, the recurrent theme and keynote of the visions; a battle to the utterance, waged between the knights and the insects, of which Basil was both spectator and steward of the lists. The urgency for this was brought home to him one night, when he got up to satisfy a certain need and lo!, in the silent dark, *toc-toc* he heard, a pulsing softer than a drum but louder than a watch, the sentence of which to his ears sounded irrevocable, as if delivered by the hoofs of a pale horse of the Apocalypse.

Trogium pulsatorium... the solemn denomination which he had learnt from his manual of book-hygiene rose to his lips.

And along with it the second baptismal name which since the times of Linnaeus had specified the little monster: Atropos. The meaning of which is. . .

Basil, it must be admitted, was of ecstatic temperament and muddle-headed, but he possessed a miraculous ear, able to catch the most minimal fibrillation in the heartbeat of sounds; and to relish within the meaning of every word the core of music which is there concealed, as in a crystal is concealed the light. Thus, to take the first examples that come to mind, such words as "Passion-flower" or "algebra", rather than referring, as in the noddles of normal people, to a flower obscurely symbolic of Christ's sufferings or a lucid method of computation, aroused in him by turns the emotions of a miserere or an alleluia, and he had only to repeat them slowly to himself to assume, instinctively, both in his gait and in his gestures, now the crestfallenness of a surrender, now the unyielding pride of a gauntlet thrown down by Reason.

This explains why the written syllables on which he had fed all these months, fat and lean, dry and moist, and with them the credentials of all his characters, and the history of their doings, rather than arranging themselves in his mind in plausible historical sequences, all jostled together like sharps and flats on a stave run amok. A sonorous hotch-potch to which – to rationalize it and give it the sanction of hard fact – this Atropos now came to add its rasping stridor. And that funereal continuous din, *toc-toc*, which certainly from this time forth would nevermore fall silent.

A suchlike knocking, Basil was at once convinced, did not proceed from the thumping of an artery rising in arms to mortify his hearing, nor from Chalchidian wind that caused the shutters rhythmically to creak. No, it was the footfalls of the fiend King Wordworm in person, the field commander and lord of the Worms, who, having scented his prey from afar, leaving other nations untouched and thereby allaying their fears with a fake armistice, had resolved to fare forth across the billows and through mountain passes to strike at the heart of the most authentic sanctuary and homeland of mankind.

At dawn the knocking ceased, and the monk set about searching with a lens in every corner of the room. To no effect: the books were manifestly in good condition, there was no sign of slaver or excrement on any piece of furniture or equipment; neither paper, nor fabric, nor wood, was broached by any wound.

At which Basil took fresh heart, persuading himself that the fiend Wordworm was but a trick of his claustral short rations. Except that the following night the *toc-toc* started again. That something had gained entrance to the fortress was now beyond all doubt. And it could only be a female, according to the instructions in his manual, for only the females pulsate in that fashion, beating their abdomens hard against some surface and thereby dispatching into the air a proposal of love. To whom, if not to a male worm present and near by? And with what in view if not a direful fecundity?

Thenceforth the monk slept not but in brief, spasmodic snatches. And in them hearing, or partly hearing, the percussion of death. Nor did awakening lessen his distress; on the contrary he prowled dog-fashion up and down the cell, scratching, sniffing, pricking up his ears, here dripping paraffin into the cracks, there out of scrupulousness sprinkling every corner with poisonous but ineffective powders. And now and then whirling round to catch the enemy unawares. But his ultimate resource was to marshal his heroes in the lists. Their forms, one at a time, he moulded in the air with both his hands, or called forth from the stains and shadowy patches of the chamber in the guises of sword-bearing angels, that they should flock to exterminate the invading army in the twinkling of an eye. Don Quixote and D'Artagnan, Ajax and Roland, the Princes Bolkonsky and Homburg, all in a body – paladins, musketeers, knights-templar – paraded before him, a pageant of gallantry and derring-do, the garrison of God on earth. Othello commanded the fleet, Samson the infantry, El Cid led the cavalry; and in their wake tourneys and torches, battle-cries, fanfares, the throes of death, with the Heroes by some magic wand belittled to infinitesimal puppets, the Worms aggrandized to equal them in stature, as in some double, reciprocal trick with mirrors.

When night fell, from the screen of the wall the battle shifted to his eyes. Closed, these were, but not so tight that between his lids he could not glimpse a moon that bedazzled the chamber through a window. And in a shaft of it, as myriad dust-flecks dance in a sunbeam, eddies of milky globulets astir, astral disembodiments of oblivion. The sensation was that of advancing on shipboard encircled by dead calm at night, when the water is like shot silk uncloven by the prow: a changeful and vaporous mirage contending with the twinkling immensity of the stars. At which Basil was visited by tears of sweetness, felt suddenly brim-full of peace. It was time to lead his champions by the hand into the white tents to sleep; time for even him to drowse for a minute. For a minute... Then, once again, *toc-toc.*

One morning, during the routine scrutiny, the famous Bible of Borso d'Este revealed an unequivocal portent: a tunnel, noticeable only on opening the volume at the right page, ran from the spine towards the interior and up the white margin, until it sinuously encroached upon the text. Superficially for now, and with this peculiarity: that the insects appeared to have chiefly aimed at eroding the proper names in the text, as if in them, and not in the hair of the head or the soles of the feet, resided the strength of a hero. And craftily they began at the end, where the blood flows murkier and less discerning. With the result that on the venerable parchment few were the sovereigns and warriors who were not docked and mangled, reduced to a mere initial of tenuous identity, an S for Saul, nothing but an M for Moses...

Utterly aghast, Basil hastened to inspect the remaining envelopes. Alas, the assault had been simultaneous and fierce, and the traces of it were ubiquitous, resembling the crumbs from an enormous meal, or the chips and shavings under a carpenter's workbench. Page after page Basil reviewed the volumes, numbered the scattered limbs of his vanquished legion. Severed from their torsos the busts remained, to crumble into dust, each one where the fangs had seized it in its sleep. Nor was there any hope but that even they, themselves chewed up and bolted down, would soon altogether vanish...

The novice reddened, a purple flush overspread his virtuous tonsure, overlaid the wine-coloured birthmark that disfigured his face. What to do? Into the creases of the volumes, along the grooves of the craters, he pried with his strongest lens to find the aggressors. And find them he did. Bristling with hairs, mailed with scales, he saw them busying about like ants, drawn up in columns and bent on destroying whatever remnants of a person they might meet in the lines, where the hallowed ink of the centuries was putting up a fight. Some had fallen, run through on the brim of the captured trench (for the victims, it must be said, had sold their lives dearly), but the remainder – ah, how many! – swarmed in every direction and, where paper lacked, cannibalistically scrunched up one another. In the mêlée one stood out, larger, more bloated, cylindrical, vivid orange. He must be the great chief, King Wordworm in person, tackling the loftiest citadel of all: the first page of Genesis, where God creates the heavens and earth. Basil thought in his fuzzy way that the heavens and the earth existed because that Name existed there in that text, and that to erase it was tantamount to erasing everything. He peered at King Wordworm through his lens. The monarch was reclining in momentary repose on a heap of rubble – vowels and consonants – his wings crossed on his belly. Wings, did I say? In reality ultra-fine bristles, perishable tissues inadequate to conceal a single one of the brownish warts on the body, at the extremities of which, even in that state of quiescence, ceaselessly crackled his interminable antennae. Basil attempted to squash him with a heavy iron pin, but he wriggled free and vanished at high speed along the col formed by the spine of a folio. What to do? The war was lost. Unless... unless...

Into Basil's mind there floated a scrap of lore he had learnt from Brother Macarius when they were together preparing the first defences. Regarding this freshly minted race of worms, these ink-sucking vampires, Brother Macarius was wont to repeat that one viand alone was effectual in diverting them from papyri and incunabula, one for which they were immeasurably gluttonous: and this was honey. Of which Basil possessed, as emergency rations, a row of brimming vessels. He stripped naked, retaining on his body nothing but his crucifix, brought down the jars from the loft, smeared every inch of himself with the entire contents, and stretched out motionless on the tiled floor. The familiar *toc-toc* was shortly heard approaching, thousands of ticklesome trotterlets were trotting all over him. He waited thus for hours, until certain of having lured on to his person the entire enemy population. He then sprang to his feet, threw wide the window, vaulted the sill, and cross in fist and cry on lips plunged headlong into the Aegean.

The Sleuth

UNTIL JUST THE OTHER DAY I thought it the finest profession in the world. Healthy, exciting, manly. A recreation for
the intellect, a panacea for the constitution. No more grumps,
flatulence or uric-acidity, but wellbeing tingling beneath the
skin, as after a shower or a satisfactory defecation. I hoofed it
from dewy morn to dusky eve, fell into sleep as trusting as a
babe, and eight hours later opened to the light two eyes full of
fresh curiosity and a mind uncluttered and fertile.

What more can I tell you? I wedded the joys of tourism to
those of espionage, I was at once a confessor of consciences and
a director of destinies, a globe-trotter and a god. And paid
good money, what's more: a regular salary from "Long-Range
Binoculars", the firm I worked for, plus tips when the case was
wrapped up, the latter often extremely generous, the lavish-
ments of relief or of desperation; that is, of two excessive
emotions conducive to prodigality.

I was in the boss's good books. He was the famous Marullo,
former chief reporter on the crime pages of the *Town Crier*, at
the entrance to which he had found me one morning fishing
for a job as a trainee-assistant from a group of journalists in
transit towards the bar. "I'll bring you the missing finger of
the Mangled Woman," I was bragging. "An interview with the
cut-throat of Acquacetosa, the snap of His Cardinal Eminence
surprised on the lap of Spartacus the Fatman. I'll bring you...
I'll bring you..."

The rest of them had a good laugh at my expense, all high

and mighty and convinced they were going to set the world to rights with fountain-pens poised like Toscanini's baton. But not Marullo. He took me seriously and sent me straight to the front line – right then and there, just in from the provinces, smutty from the train-journey and bleary-eyed from a sleepless night. Callow in limb and callow in lingo, but braggart enough to win him over. Years later, when he had retired, he took me under his wing in the agency he had set up to maintain his young mistress, and I became both lenses of his "Long-Range Binoculars".

I possess, if not all the professional skills of the private eye, at least the greatest of them, which is circumspection and the art of self-erasure, of disappearance. This has not prevented me from having printed, for publicity reasons, an exuberant visiting card with my credentials in black and white, *Benito Ciuffo, Private Investigator*, and at the foot, like an epigraph, a line of Ceccho Angiolieri's I learnt at school: "I could follow a madman all day long. . ."

"It's whims such as this," said Marullo approvingly, "that impress clients, and enable one to double the tariff." And indeed, from that time on, there hasn't been a husband who, turning my rectangle of stout cardboard this way and that, has failed to gratify me with a look half incredulous and half jubilant, as if being offered omnivision in easy monthly instalments.

Yes, I started out by tailing adulterers: it's the easiest and least risky kind of training. One is up against totally innocent antagonists incited by a blind and tender fever, who if they look behind them at all do so only once, at the very last moment, foot on the threshold of the garçonnière. Their sole concern, at that instant, being to scrutinize the faces of the passers-by for any that spell danger. Your own face, unknown to them, slips swiftly from their vision, less avoided than excluded. Not knowing you, they are rashly convinced of being unknown in return, and leave you safe and sound, anonymous, a witness shrouded in mist. For it is of the essence in a sleuth to assume clothing, features and gestures wholly anonymous and repetitive, exact replicas of those of others and mutually interchanging in an ill-defined miscellany. Your height should therefore be average, your build likewise, a diet will be of assistance. Let newspapers be your allies, to spread open before your face (but put not your trust in tabloids, no bigger than handker-chiefs). Let the page you pretend to read at the bus-stop be the suspicion-lulling sports page, with a minuscule spyhole in the middle.

Until almost yesterday, therefore, it seemed to me the most wonderful trade in the world. An active, open-air life, just exactly what the doctors never tire of advising me, me and my fatty acids... Not only is there more to be seen out of doors than in, but you get better value out of what meets eye and ear. For, properly considered, what is this world but an endless parade of colour, sound and motion, starting with the Big Bang, and of which there falls to us, between birth and requiem, but an infinitesimal tittle, an infinitesimal instant? Just the one, then off we go, no time to say boo or bravo from our temporary seat in the gods before – as they say where I come from – we are heads without noses, and everlasting darkness swallows us up. Sometimes when I leave my flat first thing in the morning, and see the frost melting in the sun on the flower-beds of the little garden attached to our block, or the emerald of the grass lustrous from a night of rain, there rises to my lips the saying so dear to Marullo: *Nocte pluit tota, redeunt spectacula mane...* and I think for the nonce that I'm on my way to a theatre, but that for me, as for everyone, the playbill has reserved but a single matinée, and the other performances are none of my business. Except that I, Benito, have an advantage over the rest in the profession I exercise: that of enquiring more closely, for as long as the curtain is raised, into this tangle of shadows on the wall of Plato's cave. Doesn't "investigate" mean to try to

see more, to learn more? And if on top of that they pay me
money for it. . .

Well then, after such an honoured career, with Marullo more a
partner and father than a boss, after being so much in love with
my work as to practise it even on Sundays as a hobby, tailing
people picked at random from the crowd and trying to ascertain
their works and days for the sole purpose of interweaving their
mystery with the cross-threads of my own imagination. . . Well
then, after such a career, for some time now I have been troubled
by doubts as to whether the very ground of the terms, the causes
and effects, on which I have so far confidently encamped, is
not becoming porous, crumbly, unstable; if, in a word, my
presumption that I am a living being is not showing signs of
the inner gnawings of a loathly worm. Must I come out with
it? I am faced with no new sight or event but two little words
ring out in my brain-pan, there to re-echo inextricably: *true* and
false, *false* and *true*. . . A fickle hallucination of sounds, prejudicial
to an enquiry, and one which vainly I implore to confine itself
to a single channel rather than flitting hither and thither among
fantasies, among phantoms!

At which I am reminded of the game my boss and I have
invented for slack afternoons when the telephone languishes. A
game of agreeable fatuity, to wit:

He starts off with a title or saying, the first that comes to
mind. For example, just to stick to union rules, "secret agent".
To which I reply with another dual concept which uses one
word, or develops the verbal root of one element, and then
introduces a new one, for example (taking "agent"), "act of
God." He, picking up the newcomer, counters with "God willing." I, therefore: "Where there's a will there's a way." Upon
which he starts to sing, "Way down upon the Swannee River,"
to which I riposte with "Down by the riverside. . ." And so on
until one of us, unable to add a link to the chain, gives up.

In no wise diverse is the feeling I have about existence,

especially while waiting at a café table for some he or she over-due to emerge from the doorway opposite. It is the feeling of a machine constructed of transient puffs of air, distorting mirrors, spurious kinships; or a preposterous reticulation falling apart on all sides, with no tangible steel cable to bind together the split links and meshes. Must we therefore wait for death, to account for life? When lights are fled and garlands dead and of the fairground nothing is left but doleful newspapers in the mud and the ruts of cartwheels; when of so many almanacs, identikits, traffic signs, of so many whys and wherefores, silence is the sole and only heir? A bitter thing it is, here below, to be unable to decide between sense and nonsense, between the gigantic jigsaw with billions of pieces that yet, each clicked into place, would describe a most beautiful function, if not the effigy and name of a God; and the non-functioning machine-monster, the Great Amorph that proliferates from itself, the compass that madly whirls to every wind of the wind-rose... Unable to decide, I say, yet to trudge along like this, castle-building and foot-slogging to no avail, following blissfully unaware ladies and gentlemen, the make-believe ends of a skein I kid myself I am unravelling and that is really unravelling me...

This said, do I have to add that my pet vice of shadowing people combines, as do all vices, remorse with pleasure? The fact of worming my way into a story that is not mine, while at first it threw me into ecstasies of power, now prompts me to obscure misgivings. As in these midwinter days on the trail of my present quarry. He is a skinny fellow with clothes a shade too big for him, though worn with old-fashioned flair. A few wisps of white hair sprouting from beneath a soft felt hat, the rolling gait of a sailor lately come ashore. To all appearances a walkover of a case: he has not an inkling that he *is* a case at all. I pick him up each morning at his regular news kiosk and escort him round, to the Villa, to the Corso, follow him through curious mazes and meanderings, inexplicable pauses, suspect accelerations, in

the neighbourhoods between the Piazza and the river. But while
I am following him, every so often snapping him with my miniature camera, I am intrigued by an odd mannerism, seeing him
suddenly stop dead at a corner and poke his nose out, investigate
something or other in front of him, and then proceed, with
caution or alacrity as the case may be, but always with an air of
testy attentiveness. The worst of it is that he is not concerned
about me being on his tail, but with certain other persons or
things that he can see and I can't. Until, with dusk already
falling, we turn into a deserted straight in the suburbs, and I
keep right in to the wall, flatten myself against the shop
windows, but am none the less able to distinguish, four blocks
ahead, the silhouette of a fat man in black striding along in
front of us; one who, if he crosses the street from one pavement
to the other, gives a slight sideways twist as if expecting a car
to appear out of nowhere. Or as if. . .

Where are we going, I ask myself, the three of us, like three
naïve Curiatii, to die? Cat's-paw to both, I press them close
at heel on felt-shod feet, but I have lost all ambition to be
huntsman-in-chief. The moon assists me by hiding behind a
cloud. When it reappears I have already gained the safety of a
wedge of shadow. Safety in a manner of speaking. . . For the
fat man in the distance has frozen beneath a traffic-light. So has
the skinny one between us. Me too, without a sound. But
behind me I catch the scrape of a boot on paving, as of one
who has halted an instant late, or stumbled. I move again when
the others move, stop when they stop. But each time the limping
step behind me repeats its miscalculation. By now I can no
longer doubt it: I am following someone who is following
someone. But someone is following me. Not even bothering to
hide. And search me who it could be.

The Purloiner of Memories

From the parish priest of S... to the bishop of T...

RIGHT REVEREND and Worshipful Lord, early in the winter
of the current year of 1818, in this secluded village clinging to
the nethermost crags of the Alps, in which I exercise my cure
of souls, I was made party to a matter uncommon in the extreme,
not to say prodigious, insomuch as its singularity appeared to
surpass all human understanding, and to be elucidated only by
adducing the mysteries of some superhuman will. Celestial, or
diabolical? It is not for me, humble mountain priest that I am, of
little learning and modest understanding, to presume an answer,
wherefore I confine myself to presenting howsoever much of
the tangled sleave is known to me, so that the threads of it may
be unravelled in the proper spheres.

Presenting it, I say: and already a fear assails me, of whether
it is not sacrilegious to make myself the divulger of a confession
heard under seal, albeit from the lips of an unrighteous man,
and with manifestly evil intent, and therefore, my presumption
is, entirely null and void. Let it be said that I would, in obedience to canon law, have myself hastened to open my heart in
confession in this regard, or in any case have requested dispen-
sation, as soon as I went down into town for my regular provisions. But for the fact that, being confined to bed by a curious
debility which leads me to despair of my life, and unwilling to
take the risk, in view of the present widespread floods, of travelling the roads in such a sorry plight, I have resolved not to keep

this secret to myself, to the jeopardy of innocent souls, but to entrust it under sealed cover to a kinsman of mine, in the hope that he may, overcoming the adversities of the season, humbly deliver it into the hands of Your Eminence, to whose bene-volence I commend my soul.

Let what comes of it be as Heaven wills. Here meanwhile, in plain words, is the occurrence.

I was in church as is my wont, one afternoon not long since, awaiting the unfailing penitents of the hour of compline, three spinster sisters, the most innocent creatures in the world, but so tetchy with their own consciences as to wish to purge them daily of the most imaginary stains. I was therefore making haste towards the confessional, where I like to be seated in good time, in part from my long-standing habit of avoiding with the believer (in view of the imminence of the Sacrament) any con-verse of homely familiarity, which might diminish the spiritual passion in us both, and in part because in that dark haven, where a single vertical streak of light seeps through the drawn curtains, I feel myself singularly docile to my zeal in God; nor is it seldom, should my parishioners tarry, that I abandon myself, not without tears, to prayer...

I had, then, barely opened the door of the confessional with my right hand than I felt my left arm seized in a feverish grip: that of an elderly man, wild-eyed, tall, with fairish hair, clad in an opulent blue frock-coat, who sprang out abruptly at my side, for in the semi-darkness of the nave I had not chanced to see him earlier. A foreigner, without a doubt, and not merely foreign to these upland parts, where for many a league around we all know each other by sight, but to the whole Italic nation, as could easily be apprehended both from the singularity of his com-plexion and his attire, and from his stiff and northern mode of speech.

Nor did I have leisure to wonder by what defiles and for what reason he had arrived here in our midst but "Come, Father," he ejaculated, "hear me under oath of secrecy!" And so saying he all but thrust me into my wooden alcove and seated himself on the prie-dieu, lowering his head so far as to bring his mouth comfortably to the level of the grating and of my hidden ear.

I was more than a little hesitant, not through any quailing of the spirit, but because in the man's speech and manner I had at once detected an anguish unchristian, reeking of pride and recalcitrant to contrition. First and foremost, therefore, I required him to recite a *Confiteor*, to no better end than to elicit a paroxysm of laughter and the following torrential spate of words:

"Father, hear me out first and thereafter inflict on me your penances. You should know that I have neither name to tell you, nor age, nor nation. Not that I do not wish to, but that I cannot. Naught do I know of myself save that I am now come from Bavaria and speak that language correctly and, though less well, your own. According to what I feel within me of my declining powers, and can judge from my face in the mirror, upon my head there must be more than threescore years and less than threescore and ten. Yet it is as if I were but three years old. Inasmuch as thus many are the years for which I have lived conscious of myself and mindful of my life; and for thus many have I gone roaming all the regions of Europe in search of my lost identity and remembrance perished. Three years, I say, three years it being since I regained my senses one morning at the foot of an escarpment which I had by I know not what mischance pitched down. My mount dead at my feet, but I in body free from hurt, were it not for a dark clot of blood at my temple, where I had struck against an outcrop of rock. At my side, sundered by the impact from the pack-saddle, lay two large saddle-bags, which not without astonishment and bewildered glee I perceived to be brim full of golden thalers. No papers about me, nor any sign to tell me who I was: a total blank and vacancy of mind, bereft of the tiniest morsel of the past. Who was I? What was I doing among those inaccessible gorges? Was

I a brigand, a merchant, a postillion, a monarch? Whither was
I bound? Whence had I come? I was not at the outset prompted
to enquire deeply, but, stunned as I was, I clambered back up
the steep, dragging the baggage behind me with a rope, confident that with the return of my strength and the dispersal of
the mists, I would once again, from my present nakedness, have
donned the garments of my baptism and my condition. I was
assisted in my journey by a youth who shortly thereafter passed
along the road on a haycart, and whom I rewarded with a few
small coins. Without saying a word with regard to myself, but
that I had been unseated by a caprice on the part of my mount,
and was now in search of an inn and a doctor in the nearest
village. I found both with perfect facility, but with no profit
in respect of gaining better cognizance of myself. The doctor
informed me, concerning the wound, that it was of little
moment, but that memory would labour no short while to
return. He counselled me, in the interim, to go in search of
any previous acquaintances from whom I might learn my identity or, at the least, an indication of some kind, a rekindling of
consciousness, as one who with a poker stirs the dying embers
and reanimates the hot blaze on the hearth.

"Thenceforth I have ceaselessly journeyed through every
region, letting myself be seen in every place, in theatres, in
market squares, on fair-days and the feast-days of saints, ever
hoping that amid the crowd a finger might be pointed and a
voice cry out a name, or a hand grasp mine. Seeing that I had
no want of money, I made a display of servants and equipages,
for I wished to pass before no man's eye without leaving my
mark. Cyprian was the name I went under, and in any assembly
of persons I all but yelled out this pseudonym in the hope of a
reminder or a denial which never came. I was soon forced to
conclude that my previous existence had passed as if writ on
water: no one appeared to have had knowledge of it. I lived,
therefore, as the simulacrum of a man amongst men, the only
nameless one in a world baptized, a foundling without a past.

Nor, hearing a distant cry of 'Cyprian!', did I turn. In a book in the German tongue I read the story of the man without a shadow, and I laughed it to scorn. How much more bitter was my destiny, on the threshold of old age and having nothing at my back but night. For not of a mere shadow had I been robbed, but of the entirety of my long life. I had lived – of that there could be no doubt – but it was as if for all those many years I had slept, and without a single glimmer of a dream. Alas, what boots it to live at all, if times past do not abide and embody themselves in us? But in *my* wake, far from it! The years were swart stones, a pit of Cimmerian rocks whence not a ghost arose, neither of the first time I had seen the sea, nor kissed the lips of woman, nor danced or walked in a park by the light of the moon. No memory was left me, of mother, of friends, of duels, of grief, of glory. Not a breath of memory, therefore not a breath of life. In pitching from that clifftop I had been murdered. So what was I now, with my new, my infant memories but three years old? What was I and who was I? Nothing survived within me but a sliver of willpower, a fruitless striving, a momentary bubbling in the blood. Whatever might betide me served not to add one brick the more to a previously erected edifice of my life, but rested on foundations of thin air. I was even as a fragment of the capital of some ravaged temple, or the one remaining note of a musical score devoured by mice. . ."

"My son," with some diffidence I interposed, "Jesus on the Last Day will recognize his own. . ."

Through the grating I heard an ejaculation, whether a laugh or a sob I know not. Then in a low voice he resumed:

"Father, my story is not yet ended. Nor would I be here to relate it to you, were I not in need of your assistance. A six-month since, a further and terrifying thing befell me. I had made my way to Dresden, drawn there by the report of a master painter who delights in painting dreams. I requested a portrait from him, being myself the mere dream of a man. He looked at me with piercing eyes and refused to paint me; indeed, he declared he had already done so years before, without so much as having met me. He thereupon showed me a canvas, depicting a wayfarer on a lofty peak, gazing at a sea of clouds and mists beneath his feet. Now, the peculiarity of that picture was that the subject thereof had his back turned to the onlooker: verily a Faceless and Nameless One – my double.

"Profoundly shaken, I left him to visit a theatre and take my mind off my infirmity. But lo! journeying homeward, already after the hour of midnight, and the carriage moving at an easy pace through the silence of the city, it so happened, after having enviously run over in my mind the scenes of the performance I had witnessed, that I fixed my eyes intently upon the nape of the coachman's neck, and at the same instant felt certain minuscule lights kindle between my eyelids and swell into the guise of a great flower, thereafter to contract into a beam of light. When I closed my eyes a tingling ferment seemed to open fanwise behind my brow, while an odour of roses pervaded the air about me. Until, on a sudden, within me surged a MEMORY. Of a boy in an orchard dangling a noose to catch a grass-snake... And others, others: of a stable-lad on a coach-box, a hostler surrounded by mules and manure; and others again: of coaching inns and of mules on precipitous pathways; then the climax, strictly contemporaneous, of a man seated on a coach-box who feels a pair of eyes from beneath the hood of the vehicle pierce agonizingly through the back of his head...

"It did not take me long to grasp the truth, and after the first brief ecstasy my blood ran cold: I had not recovered my own past but, by dint of some unthinkable mesmeric force, with the magnet of my mind had usurped that of the other. Those memories were not mine but his, I had purloined them. He and I simultaneously cried out with pain, but at that moment the horse reared; nor was the poor wretch any longer guiding it, but lay deathly pale on his back beneath his seat. I hastened to take his place on the box and return him, more dead than alive, to his family.

"What more can I add? Since then it needs only that I stare with fanatic intensity at passers-by to expropriate every vestige of their past and transfer it into my own head. With a certain woeful jubilation, but without much inclination to cry triumph. I well know I have fabricated for myself false roots, a harvest of froth. Nor can I any longer control, within myself, the brawling of such discordant memories. Willingly would I abstain from leaving so many lifeless or languishing victims wheresoever I pass, but I find no exorcism to physic me, unless thou help me. This is an ill that even more than others is destroying me, and over which I no longer have dominion. As leeches suck blood, I go likewise sucking each man's memories with my gaze. Wherefore I seek out snowy wastes and deserts, and walk with lowered eyes."

This, Your Eminence, is the man's story. To which I countered that I was not authorized to practise other than ordinary exorcism, whereas to his case the solemn rite alone seemed fitting. And still with gentle words was I striving to soothe him, and dispose him to make peace with himself, when to a question of mine I received no answer, but rather, a moment later, heard the voice of one of my three spinsters chanting the litanies beyond the grating in the accustomed manner. Whereat I perceived that the man had fled without attending succour. Fled whither, though? Therefore I tremble, reverend lord, lest he should still be at large, armed with such injurious power, among the lambs of my flock. And I tremble the more, my lord, because from that day forth I have not been well in health, but feel my brain beset by lengthy shadows; and very numerous memories, until but yesterday luminous within me, do I feel to have been amputated and bled away. On account of which I forever repeat my name, for fear of being robbed of it. Could it be that the hapless man instilled me with his humour? That I too am about to lose my memory? What then would become of my soul? Stripped of every remembrance good or bad, and therefore of

94

my very selfhood, how could I present myself to the judgement of God? And already in the room I seem to scent an odour of roses. . .

A Stroll with a Stranger

For the ten days July 4th–15th 1865 Baudelaire, hounded by credi-
tors, returned from Brussels to Paris in search of money. He failed
to obtain any, but during this brief home visit he had a curious
encounter, related below.

THE TWO HANDS POUNCED simultaneously on the same
volume. The one was small, white, well-tended, but with brittle,
greyish nails scored by fine grooves; the other – square, swarthy,
workaday – emerged hairily from the sleeve of a redingote. For
a moment no one breathed a word, the two men sized each
other up, mutually assessing their respective years and powers:
forty-five or thereabouts carried poorly versus a lightly-carried
sixty-five. Finally, "We'll have to see who needs it most," they
said with one voice, neither relaxing his grip.

"We'll have to see who's willing to pay most," put in the
bookseller equably, detaching his backside from the parapet of
the *Quai*.

He was in a minority, for the two at once agreed that a
book such as the *Mémoires* of Vidocq was not worth the bother
of an auction, and that to dispute its possession a duel of
words would more than suffice. "For the moment let us divide
the cost," suggested the older man. "We can reach an agree-
ment later, as we walk. If the worst comes to the worst we'll
toss up."

*   *   *

96

They walked on in the July sunshine, the object of their rivalry provisionally housed in a pocket of the redingote.

"My work," began the elder of the two, "is to track down thieves, to unmask murderers. These experiences of an illustrious colleague might well teach my reasoning powers some new short cuts. Inasmuch" – and here he smiled – "as Vidocq put far more faith in ruses than in reasoning. . ."

He was a man of robust build, his advancing years still sitting fresh upon him, and dressed as if for winter despite the warmth of the summer month and time of day. But his brow showed up all the drier in comparison with that of his interlocutor – deathly pale and pouring sweat – albeit the man was lightly clad.

"And I," returned the latter, "in a week's time have to give a lecture on Balzac. I need a starting-point for dealing with Vautrin." He paused. "I am a poet," he added, with a tilt of the chin. "But to make a living I am obliged to write articles, give lectures. If you could call it living. . ."

His was a head shaven and proud, the head of a galley-slave, and his voice cut through the air like a steel knife-edge. The old functionary nodded: "A poet, that goes without saying. I knew it from the start." He gestured towards the magazine under the other's arm. "Just now, at the bookstall, I observed you rummaging among the books with one hand only, clasping this paper with the other and giving it a sidelong glance every few minutes. Such is the infallible manner of poets the morning they find a poem of theirs in print." And dexterously slipping the *Petite Revue* from under the other's arm, "Here we are," said he, and in a low voice declaimed:

> *La gerbe épanouie*
> *En mille fleurs,*
> *Où Phoebé réjouie*
> *Met ses couleurs,*
> *Tombe comme une pluie*
> *De larges pleurs.*

97

He frowned. "Too damp for my rheumatics," he complained, accompanying his look with a wink and a sparkle in the eye, as if seeking a crony with whom to dupe some non-existent outsider.

"The truth is," he admitted, "I have very little ear for verse. My job is to infer and to deduce."

"My name is Baudelaire," said Baudelaire, "and I have nothing against murderers. Whereas I have a great deal against reason. I would never forgive myself if I left you the use of such a book. It might cost some impulsive drunkard his head."

They had reached the Pont de la Tournelle, heading towards the Cité. From where they stood the river appeared cram-full of craft of every shape and size, canoes, coal barges, rafts laden with logs. These so troubled and muddied the waters as to dispirit the one lone fisherman down there with rod and line, though festively on every side from a thousand flagstaffs fluttered the tricolour pennants of the imminent *quatorze juillet*.

"A strange bias," resumed the policeman. "You are more vexed by the revenging guillotine than indignant at the ripper's knife. And yet you must have read De Maistre. . ."

"I have read him and love him," replied the other. "But my hangman does not don his hood to behead poor desperate wretches. His enemies are the paunchy bourgeois, the generals of the long sabres. . ." He sneered, and added between his teeth: "The publishers, the landlords, the insolent tradesmen. . ." And with a glance at his companion, "the police-force philosophers," he concluded.

"You are unjust," murmured the other. "We keep watch that you may sleep. *Vigilat ut quiescant*: that's our motto, bestowed on us by the great Louis."

"I wish," replied the poet, "that you could manage to put my creditors to sleep."

They laughed, the book almost forgotten. They entered a café and the poet accepted a tot while their ears were filled with the din of the customers, the comings and goings, a voice from behind a newspaper: "It seems King Christian has asked for an armistice. He's a wily old fox, that Bismarck. . ."; another spouted the names of unknown women – Lucienne, Margot; a third: "She's innocent, I tell you. It wasn't La Pommarais who did it!"

Workmen crowded in and crowded out, smoking short clay pipes, their smocks sweat-stained under the armpits. On the marble table, in a dribble of absinthe, struggled a fly. Neither of them rescued it.

Now they were entering the Ile de la Cité. "Heads or tails?" proposed the older man, at the end of Pont Saint-Michel and on their way past the Morgue. He won three times running, and the book was his.

The poet was aggrieved. He insisted on having one more go, just to see. . . He lost again and gave up. "You remind me," he said, following a train of thought, "of someone who never made a mistake at this dodge. He claimed to have the secret of winning every time. He's the hero of a story I translated some time ago. By an American." He looked up at the façade of the building. "We'll go in," he decided suddenly, as if he had heard his name called. And the other followed him.

Through a carriage entrance they reached the brightly lit vestibule. Here, as they turned left, a long glass wall protected by an elbow-high barrier divided them from the exposition hall. Three rows of black slabs were to be seen, tilted slightly down towards the foot, and on each lay a corpse, face upwards and with the head cranked up and offered to view in a copper mechanism. A clothes-horse beside each corpse displayed shawls, jackets, neckties, shirts, and any other noteworthy tokens of identity.

"From Alsace," said the older man, pointing through the glass at a bundle of swollen, purplish flesh, recently fished out by the look of it. "Maidservant in a student boarding-house in the Latin Quarter. Three months pregnant. Name of Liselotte. Two failed suicides, before this one. . ."

He passed on, studying the corpses and the objects at some length before speaking.

"A corporal. Deserter. Fought in Mexico with Bazaine. Knifed in a brawl in Passy and finished off with stones. Has a clockmaker brother married to a Jewess..." He seemed to sniff the air, apparently trying to nose out a syllable or two lurking in his memory. "In La Rochelle," he added, with a trace of hesitation.

"Curse you!" cried Baudelaire. "You're not going to indulge your fancy for bowling me over! You won't see me on my knees, asking you how and why! No, I'm going to be the one to stagger you. You're a bachelor, of excellent but impoverished family, and lived for a long time in your youth on a third floor in Faubourg Saint-Germain, Rue Dunot. You have assisted the Paris police in many cases over the last twenty years, from the double murder in this very street to the theft of a royal letter. You are no longer an amateur, I see, but have joined the Force. And certainly you no longer write poetry. In a word, sir, if you are not the devil himself, your name is Auguste Dupin."

"Dupont," the devil corrected him. "Aurèle Dupont, Sub-Prefect of police of the Seine *département*. For the rest of it, I don't know what you're talking about."

London Nightpiece

DECEMBER 1ST 1887

WHAT A PEA-SOUPER! Not that he minded it. Fog for him was one garment the more, a turned-up loden collar to shield him from spying eyes, a mask behind which to vanish with impunity...

Ever since childhood when, playing with other youngsters there in Petticoat Lane, he thought nothing more fun than to sneak out from a dark corner behind some little girl's back, suddenly call her name in an assumed voice, and see her whirl round with a startled, questioning, freckly face, then make off helter-skelter, her skinny legs flailing in rolled-down stockings.

Ah, the good old days... Of which the picture remaining in his mind was one, above all, of fog. As if those years had been nothing but one long footslog through the fog, cheeks smeared with soot, between peeling walls, amid a stench of urine and herrings, while, louder than any outburst of cursing or groan of pleasure or of death-throes, one sole, persistent sound reached his ears: the inconsolable fog-horns of tug-boats on the Thames.

He pressed his forehead against the window, tried to see out. A blank, nothing but a yellowish blank. But, as he peered more intently, streaks of soot seemed to hover in that opaqueness, and a hint of motion was discernible through rifts in the murk. As when from a mountain, begirt by cloud, we espy the fringe of a wind-tousled wood or the twinkle of a stream in the valley. He knew the Thames was flowing beneath that window: he felt its presence, as of an exacting confessor and friend; but at the

101

same time he felt it offer him the comfort of a shadowy cradle into which he would be happy once and for all to sink. For a moment he pictured the scene. Enough to throw up the sash, mount the sill, let himself drop, lazily milling with his arms through the easeful, complaisant, soiled cotton wool of the air. He imagined the *plumph* of the body in the water, the silence and the chill of peace down there.

He looked away, crossed the room to the other window, the one overlooking the docks. Not a sign of life, the city was dead, nothing more than a corpse embalmed in grimy bandages. Not even the familiar rumble of wheels on the flagstones: the hackney-carriages were all holed up for sure in sheds and livery-stables. Only a wavering lamp from time to time appeared, and was swallowed up. Doubtless some linkman, disgruntled at finding no clients to escort for a shilling through the maze of lanes. Unless it was a police patrol...

He wiped his forehead with the back of his sleeve. Although the fire was dying in the stove, and the room struck slightly chill, he was sweating. A swig of gin, gulped down neat from a bottle, did him no good. He even felt it go to his legs a little. He sat down in the old arm-chair, he almost dozed off.

In a chair as massive as this, its arms worn shiny by many elbows, his father used to take his midsummer afternoon naps. In the whole of Petticoat Lane it had no equal, perhaps, nor was there any that more resembled a throne. Fitting for his father, who was of massive build: a bull of a man. For his mother too, who was a lioness... How many Saturday nights, from his truckle-bed in the passage, he had heard them clash and mingle their mighty physiques in a duel with no quarter. Then followed a silence as of death, and tears rose to his eyes; and then he slept, and in tears he awoke. But the following day was fun. Setting off in their Sunday best for a jaunt around the nobs' part of town. The three of them in line abreast like soldiers, stopping every hour at a different pub to knock one back, careful not to lose sight of each other in the torrent of people seething in the streets, deafened by the uproar of jalopies, cabs, handcarts and bright-painted omnibuses with the passengers seated fan-wise, the lowest on the short step that almost brushes the ground, the highest with their heads on a level with the first-floor balconies, high enough to fly. Fun to watch the steam-boats on the river shooting the bridges and dipping their funnels as if making a bow, and the trains clattering sonorously over the viaducts. While below, in the main stream, escorted by boats, pontoons and rafts of every shape and size, a fleet of regal vessels processed downstream. Fun, and scary too, to creep down into the tunnel from bank to bank, step by step to go down the spiral staircase, venture into the iron intestine and emerge into the sun at the foot of the great Tower... Since then he had never been back, but had dreamt of it a thousand times, a thousand times descended into just such a shaft of pitchy filth, lantern in hand, by a stair without a handrail spiralling and spiralling upon itself...

Memorable Sundays. But among them one most vivid, vermillion in memory, paling all the rest and striking anguish to his heart: that morning when he came running and threw wide the half-closed kitchen door and beheld his mother, naked, dripping, terrible to behold, rising from the bathtub...

He passed a hand over his eyes, got to his feet, turned to take stock of the room. A humble room, but spick and span for all that. Had it not been for the professional bidet half hidden by a screen, and the smell of cosmetics heavy in the air, it could have been a young girl's room, with that stuffed bird that had lost one eye and stared from a shelf at visitors with the other, the patched doll in a corner, dressed in green, leaking tow from the head, the virginal cotton frocks and modest felt hats that cluttered the clothes-stand, the sewing bag...

He raised his eyes: the oil-lamp hanging on its wire from the ceiling, jostled in the course of the struggle, was still swinging, throwing ever-slower scrawls of light and shadow on the wall until, steadied by his hand, it ceased altogether and cast its wonted, friendly gleam on the table laid beneath it. Unnoticed before, a supper was waiting on the table, steaming hot. He removed the cover and from it rose a homely fragrance of erstwhile happiness, a remembrance of shining noons, of light-some, long-dead voices, a prattle irretrievable and heart-rending, as is every minute that passes, happy or otherwise; a memory of tall windows opening on to shop signs, shop-fronts, barrel-organs and flags merry in the wind; and a sky mysteriously blue through the glass of an empty tankard raised up to the light. . .

He was tempted. He dug a tin teaspoon into the pudding, raised it to his mouth, vomited at once on to the tablecloth. . .

But it was time to go. He washed his hands and forearms at the sink, scraping long with his pocket-knife around the edges of his nails until the last red flake had disappeared. Then Jack stepped over the bundle of hacked flesh humped across the threshold, opened the door gently, and with soft steps passed out into the night.

Don Quixote's Last Ride

GOVERNED BY SLACK REINS and irresolute spurs, Rosinante was homeward bound. And he would have been bewildered at every crossroads had he not been assisted, as his sole compass and lodestone, by the remembrance of his stable of yore. A dim remembrance, if the truth be told, since in these last years the horse had so much travelled and endured, far beyond his natural due, as to feel a stranger among the dusky vine-shoots and golden yellow thistles of La Mancha, at one time so familiar.

Nevertheless, drawn by what exiguous odour of home still abided in his nostrils, the aged hack put one hoof before the other, with precisely the gait of those cardboard quadrupeds on wheels, which parade at Carnival-time between two rowdy banks of crowd. Ambling skew-wise, tongue and ears lolling, his eye lack-lustre as if bleared by fog. . . what wonder that no exploit he could recollect availed to mitigate his wrung withers? That on the contrary, though indeed they were glorious, only the croppers he had come returned to mind; as when, spurred at full tilt against a caitiff, he was laid low by a stumble together with his beloved burden; or when felled to the ground, now clubbed by muleteers, now stoned by galley-slaves, now smitten in the lists by the Knight of the White Moon. . .

Rosinante, then, was homeward bound across the plain of Montiel, alternating with those of the donkey his posterior exhalations; and these by no means trumpeting and bold, as on the day when they set forth together, but plaintive and meek like the sighs of a penitent.

The master... ah, his appearance was changed in equal measure. Not because his neck was scored by deeper trenches, or his brow by more meandering furrows, but on account of an unprecedented whiteness that blanched his mustachios, hitherto jet-blackly pendent on either jowl. Moreover, the movements of the man seemed drained of spirit, and bereft of mettle, as if a dethroned king walked abroad in his attire.

Very different to behold was the figure of Sancho Panza riding close beside him and rapidly blinking his eyes with the air of one who has this moment ceased from staring at the sun. Albeit certain esoteric gestures and tokens left no doubt that in his mind he was maturing the expectations of a comeback, not to say a triumph: with such swift joy did his hands flit over his paunch, there to finger a belt swollen with hypothetical gold, or to identify this or that casket in the saddlebags, or to raise the wineskin to his lips for an assiduous kiss... But more so, even, on account of a new and unexpected pride in challenging the wind chin up, and in gesturing with those hands of his as if grasping an invisible sceptre... Save that but a moment later he must perforce return to using them for the most servile tasks. As when, plumb in the middle of a rickety bridge over a gorge, in the neighbourhood of Montesinos, his ass stopped dead and refused to budge, so that the yokel was obliged to relieve him not merely of his own bulk, but also of the packsaddle and paraphernalia. Nor was Rosinante to be outdone, for his legs buckled beneath him, powerless to sustain the effort of proceeding further.

"Master," said Sancho, addressing the knight, who without a word had uprooted himself from the saddle and stood apart, leaning on a flimsy rope handrail, gazing down into the chasm at the headlong waters, "Master, here we cannot abide." And so saying, seeing him thus lifeless, he unfastened the sword from his side, unsheathed it, and with the point of it went prodding the two beasts in the ribs, when he did not thwack them with the flat. Nor did he desist until he had forced them to shift and gain the head of the bridge, where he himself, with the strength of his arms and back, saw to curtailing the weight of their burdens, while his companion, still distrait and seemingly rapt, bending over the enticements of the depths, in a low voice spoke and gave himself reply:

"Quixada Quixote," he said, "what hast thou done with thy life? Lo, through fire and through ice hast thou traversed the terrestrial globe, to the behoof of gentlewomen and of the afflicted, thereby attaining trifling successes but suffering many a buffet and guffaw. Wizards have wholly sorcerized thy thought, nor canst thou any longer tell whether thou art Quixote or Quixada, whether that which views thee from the looking-glass is thine own face or an illusion, a body of flesh and blood or an aery phantom. Helmets hast thou seen change places with brazen basins, inns with castles; on the chin of a smooth-skinned barber sprout a fantastic beard; from the sallet of a paladin arise the surly features of a curate ... Ye also, Maritornes, Altisidora, my goddesses in masquerade, and thou Dulcinea, daybeam of my darkness, glory of mine affliction, all, all of ye, through what a multitude of spells and disenchantments have ye wrought confusion in my heart, now queens now serving-wenches, odorous now of garlic now of civet, but ever in an instant fleeting, when with vain hand I strove to hold ye back... Alas and alack, a chimera and a cozenage is life, a gaming-table raised in the great *plaza* of the world. And love is a tangle that by now I despair of unravelling, unless it be in the spumings of this stream..."

But now with importunate haste Sancho was summoning him, dragging him away by the arm, with the air of a pugnacious nurse, a liberty such as at one time he would never have allowed himself. At which the hidalgo in mournful tones complained:

"I'faith, thou play'st the too-brusque arbiter, laying hold on me in such a manner. Dost think thyself e'en now upon the island, and crowned King Sancho the First, invested with rights to use main force upon every subject in thy dominions?"

To which the squire: "This is no time to stand on ceremony, friend Quixote, for the boards beneath our feet are rotten. And it falls to my lot to see and foresee for two. You know that when the blind lead the blind both fall together. Come nigh me of a soft pace. You will know e'er long whether I have not exercised good husbandry, and have not increased in wisdom and merit, so far as to lay claim myself to blazon of knighthood. But just now think of your life. 'If you go chasing two hares together, You miss the one and lose the other.'"

Thus they escaped those straits, nor had they the heart to straddle their spent mounts, the which would have ill supported them. Wherefore they went on foot, having disposed their baggage on a barrow found by happy chance by the wayside, and which Sancho, having looped his wrists to the shafts, hauled along behind him.

It was not long before Don Quixote felt his feet smarting with blisters and a powerful weakness in his chest. This notwithstanding, on he went. Albeit with his fingers he groped for Rosinante's tail and clasped it like the tresses of a loved-one, leaning upon it, eyes closed, and finding in that most loving among animals sufficient residual vigour and loyal compassion as to permit the march to continue. Until, in a rougher stretch, where the feet of innumerable goats had pitted the ground, they being but a short distance from the *Venta de l'Agua Dulce*, his strength failed him entirely and he slid gently down on to the grass.

When he recovered his senses he was in a bed in the inn, close by a window through which he discerned a patch of sky and a corner of the courtyard, where serving-maids were busy, some plucking a goose, others armed with buckets and a-chatter round the well. There was no one in the room, and our knight felt much relieved. He was not in a mood for importunate solicitudes, but took pleasure in overhearing from below, muted by the walls, those womanish jests and conversings. He sounded his body out, finding it free of wounds and bruises, but weary as it had never been after any of his thousand misfortunes. Weary with a weariness new to him, in which an intimation of undefined happiness was not altogether lacking; such happiness as he had once experienced as a boy, when after a lengthy tertian, one midday he had felt himself free at last of fever, and had leant out over the sill with cupped hands to receive the gold-red flood of the sunlight. He felt that on this present occasion he was close to dying, and that death is the remedy for life, and that this present languor was, rather than a portent of sickness, the token of an imminent convalescence. He remembered the encounter he had had, on leaving Toboso, with the actors' cart, and how Death had appeared to him, together with an unarmed Cupid, standing upright on the boards; and how a devilish Fool, jingling bells and waving inflated bladders, had fled away on Sancho's ass. That time he had easily persuaded himself that those apparitions were not what they appeared to be, but what they said they were: not Death, the Devil, and Love at all, but strolling players, mere penniless vagabond maskers.

But if that were not the case? What if they had really been, there at the outset of his journey, Death, the Devil and Love, trying to communicate an omen? It was not the first time he had seen the truth disguise itself as truth in order to make believe it was a lie. Nor was he unaware of what little worth are the eyes against the illusions of the Great Conjuror...

He arose, his lanky frame creaking inside the copious night-shirt in which someone had dressed him during his deliquium, and which gave him the semblance of a scarecrow. Thus attired he approached the window to obtain a better view, and on the instant observed the nostrils of Rosinante rise towards him from below the sill, and from the courtyard heard a friendly neigh that echoed through the room like a volley of musketry. He opened the casement and reached down to the animal's damp muzzle, but scarcely had he brushed it than he drew back, fearful lest indiscreet eyes might catch him in so unmartial a uniform; or that Sancho, made cognizant of his awakening, might come to disturb his tranquillity. He therefore returned to curl up on his pillow, pressing his bony knees together beneath the covers to create a little warmth, and from that position, insofar as they were visible, he studied the clouds in the sky, their skirmishings and passions.

An uncommon spectacle. Especially for the skies of La Mancha, whence never falls a raindrop, but which are ever painted an unyielding blue. Except that on that day the clouds of all the skies in the world appeared to have made a rendezvous there aloft, as if in a Last Judgement of clouds, and each had to find room at the expense of others, and with the others came to fisticuffs, and grappled in inextricable clinches. . .

"*Quam sordet tellus cum coelum aspicio*," murmured the knight, who in his saddlebag carried not only the stories of Amadis of Gaul, but a little book of St Ignatius. "*Cum coelum aspicio. . . Cum coelum aspicio. . .*," he repeated, like a soporific cradle-song; then, passing his hand across his brow, he shut out all deep thoughts from it, and let his eye play with the clouds after the manner of a child.

And he saw them as prodigalities of flowers, trophies of jasmines and of lilies from which a hidden hand was eternally plucking the petals. . . Or disintegrating mountain ranges, crumbled by an inward sigh, an entenderment and warmth, where streams were born, the torrents of spring, and harmless avalanches of powdery snow. . . Or a city of castles with bastions curiously carved, their drawbridges raised over dizzying moats, and among them cherubim on the wing, each bearing at his side a flaming Durendal. . . Or fearsome lions and griffins locked in duels with impalpable teeth and claws, fleecy creatures reshaped each instant by the hand of Proteus. . . Or alabaster tabernacles. . . Or flotillas of swans, forests of nymphs, the flowing tresses of Dulcinea. . .

Soon a gilded tumult began to thrill tenuously behind the curtain of immaculate percale. The sun must have risen some while ago, though only now, his finger to his lips, and with the steps of a soft-footed ghost, did he dare to enter in person, secretly, from his stage-set on the far side of the sky, to sport behind the back of all that milky whiteness. Secretly yes, but not so much so that some sleight of his presence was not discernible, an illusory milling of doubloons on a stream-bed, which the eye catches and loses at once to the refractions of an eddy. The knight stretched out his arms towards that distant gold-hoard, where the density of cloud thinned out, frayed into fugitive cirrus, O great Sun! And it seemed to him that a single cloud of disproportionate vastness had assembled, from the many minuscule clouds there had been before, and that it stretched from end to end of the horizon in the shape and form of a vessel putting to sea. As if those sports and pastimes, metamorphoses and combats, had been nothing more than preliminary exercises for the launching of this ship, and voyaging in her. Ah, to take ship, high on some Milky Way, some rainbow's end, as when astride Clavileno he had been whirled up among the stars!...

He was unable, possibly unwilling, to seize the chance. A flash of raging fire burst in the heart of the cloud and shattered it, as the sword-thrust sunders the heart of a bull in the arena. The leafy branch above the tavern door, Rosinante's harness, the hunting-knife in a servant's hand, the fleeting wing of a mayfly: the whole world turned to blood. And in that bloodlit world the edges of all things, objects or ideas as maybe, seemed to shine forth more limpid, bare and final...

Don Quixote dried his eyes with a corner of his nightshirt, leisurely resumed his weapons, leisurely vacated the room and descended on his own two feet to the courtyard. It was time to be home; Sancho would certainly have fed and groomed the animals...

He found him outside the kitchen, an orator of miracles, discoursing from the top of a stack of logs to an assembly of carters and scullions, some seated on the ground, others on the sides of their carts, but all of them hearkening in raptness and wonder. Sancho had donned the black flame-painted mantle, gift of the duchess, and stood like a tower, his eyes alight with regal fire, while his words, unhampered by their wonted clumsiness, rose up like wafting banners.

"Behold me," said he, "a servant, a peasant, by the look of me. Yet have I performed the exploits of a hero. Nor would I have believed as much before my eyes were unsealed, when I lived content with my dish of olives, ignorant of books, and every line of writing looked to me like a train of inky ants... But now I have travelled much, much fought, much suffered. Now at last I know who and what I am: a chronicle and living force of famous days... Of what a host of them could I related the tale! Yea, of that day when, vanquished by the sorcery of kings, in a palace to all appearances resembling an inn such as this, I was obliged more than once to be tossed into the air on a mule-blanket... Of when with a mere shout I put to flight the famous Gines de Pasamonte... Or of when I was given the government of an archipelago, and so well did I govern it, righting all wrongs and redressing all injuries, as to deserve the mitre which I deputed, in indignant humility, to the head of my ass. My ass, I say, but rather I should say my Pegasus, since mounted on his back I have so often taken wing, guiding him at will with two mere taps of the heel! Together we have traversed sierras and plains, we have met with princesses and goat-girls, we have made the dead to rise... You ask, what have I gained from such great ado? Only one certitude, but that immense: that I erred in trusting in my senses as a man both gross and puny. For now I know that every wretchedness of the flesh may conceal a heavenly host. And that those beings I beheld one morning, arcane monsters whirling in the air against the rim of the horizon, thirty, forty of them – who could number those monsters my master tilted at so bravely? – were, I now know, veritable and mountainous giants, Enceladus, Typhon, many-armed Briareus; and that well it warranted the hazard of defying them even to the death..."

But Don Quixote, who had heard him unobserved behind his back, "Sancho, come to your senses," gently he said. "They were only windmills. Windmills, nothing but windmills." And he whistled up Rosinante.

A Bench in the Park

First Day

HE DECIDED TO TAKE a book along, out of force of habit, although he knew he would never open one again. The doctor had been brief and brutal: "Retina irreparably damaged. Total blindness round the corner..."

"Years or months?"

"Months. Depending on whether you..."

He had nodded. He would be a model patient, and eke it out, what little light was left... He thought of another, less recent sentence, the graph of an electrocardiogram – no trouble in deciphering that one: he was pretty good at it by now. And he derived a certain wry amusement from the sporting odds on his heart or his eyesight conking out first. A neck-and-neck finish, as the papers say... though the heart was still in the lead, after a flying start. For ages now it had been quaking in his chest – it would take but a puff to topple it.

He recalled that his father, feeling the end near, had insisted on having his shoes put on before death swelled his feet. He had wanted a decent burial and had got one. But what of himself?

Villa Bellini, in the early part of the morning, could almost be taken for private gardens. A dozing, deserted enclosure undisturbed these days even by the clippety-clop of an invisible horseman from over the hedge of the former riding-school. Just the odd old-age pensioner around the edge of the large open

114

"Circus", here and there a nanny and her charge sauntering round the swan-lake, a vendor of sunflower-seeds and a balloon-man seated like surly sentries at the foot of the pathway up to what they called "Celebrities' Walk". Here, on a bench, the old man was seated, his unopened book on his knee, straining his eyes, if not to make out the date (January 16th? 18th?) bedded out in flowers, at least to piece together the salient features of the young woman and the little boy now swimming into his ken. Even when they were right in front of him he had to fumble his specs on before he could extract from those foggy blobs some resemblance to living beings. Since his eyes were so insubordinate, he called his other senses to his aid – he sniffed the air, sharpened his sense of hearing.

"Who are they?" he heard the little boy ask the girl, while bouncing his ball in a game of his own, on his own.

"Who are who?"

"Those stone heads." The boy pointed to the busts with their resolute whiskers.

"Important men. Dead men."

"Dead? What does dead *mean*?"

"Oh, run away and play, do!" exclaimed the girl, and pushed him from her. Then, plugging in the earphones of her Walkman she appeared to immure herself within its shelter, alone with a dance-tune the undivulged rhythms of which she tapped out with her toe.

The boy tossed his ball, chased it to right between the old man's shoes. And that was how the two became acquainted.

The old man is about seventy, his clothes are cheap but decent, with a few gracefully old-fashioned embellishments – a floppy bow-tie, a broad-brimmed hat, a grey waxed-canvas umbrella like that of a farm bailiff, which almost does him duty as a crutch.

The boy is tiny even for his age, which isn't much in any case, five at the outside. A blond forelock falls over a pair of

115

blue eyes, and his is the fair complexion of an aristocrat: he might be an Infante of Spain. He is talking to his ball, cajoling it, rebuking it. Especially now that it has lodged itself between the old man's massive shoes, held fast as between the pincers of a scorpion. The boy at last addresses the old gent: "Hey, please, mister!"

The old man's eyes are closed. He seems to see nothing, hear nothing. So the boy wriggles his way on hands and knees between the two legs and emerges triumphant, prize in hand. Just as he is about to make off he hears himself addressed by a name other than his own.

"Giovanni!"

He turns back. "My name's not Giovanni," he says stubbornly.

"Michele!"

"My name's not Michele." But, as the game begins to take his fancy, "You're not even *warm* yet!" And, "You're still cold, you're still cold!" he cries in answer to the old man's fishing in the dark with "Luigi? Alfio? Giuseppe?" Until the young woman, who has followed the scene from a distance, arrives and solves the matter once and for all with "Gaetano. Tano. That's his name." Then, "May I sit here, please?"

She had unplugged her earphones, and looked quite defence-less but cocky in her mannishly-cut mackintosh, the skin taut over her cheekbones and eyes with a hint of troubled urgency in them, as of one who has some pressing concern but can't find the words to express it.

She didn't wait for an answer, but sat down at the old man's side. Not only that but, taking the book from his hand, "What's that you're reading?" she asked, using a familiar *tu* which the old man accepted gratefully, seeing no flattery in it, but merely a feeling of spontaneous connivance.

"I can't read any longer. My sight's gone phut. But I bring a book along all the same, just for company. It was to this very bench that I came to do my studying when I was young. That's why whenever I come back here I bring a book."

116

"Whatever is it? Double Dutch?" said the girl, flipping over the pages.

"It's Greek," he told her. "Once upon a time I used to teach Greek. . ." But she wasn't listening any more. She had sprung up to meet a dark, stocky youth just then entering the Walk.

The boy returned from a scamper with a "Where's Nanny?", and the old man set to playing the guessing-game again.

"You mean Luisa?"

"You're cold, you're cold!"

"Concetta? Serafina? Lucia?"

"Naomi," revealed the boy generously. And added, "I love her."

"As much as your mummy, or more?" the old man asked.

The boy didn't answer at once. He was watching the vagaries of his ball on the uneven gravel.

"My mummy's dead," he said at last. "What does it mean?"

"What does what mean?"

"Dead, the dead, those people up there." And he pointed to the worn stone busts of Domenico Tempio and Mario Rapisardi.

"Dead," said the old man, "means when you can't see colours any more, can't hear sounds. When you stop moving and just stay still. Like your ball. If you don't keep it rolling it stops and stays still."

As he spoke he peered in the direction of the pair of young-sters, the youth and the girl, wrangling heatedly at the far end of the Walk. He thought he vaguely saw something pass from the man to the girl and something pass back. He realized it would be kinder not to spy, and he turned his attention to Gaetano's new game with his ball: bouncing it, pinning it to the ground with a quick flick of the foot, then, lying prone, head propped on hands, gazing steadily at its inertness.

"What are you up to now?"

"It's dead." And the boy gazed steadily on at the motionless ball before him.

In the meantime Naomi had returned, alone. She stood wringing her hands. "Whatever shall I do?" Then, under her breath, "I'll kill myself I will. Easier that way."

"Easy as winking," said the old man.

And the three of them were silent for a while.

"How old are you?" resumed the old man. Only then had he noticed her bandaged wrists, but he gave no sign of it, merely cleaning his glasses between forefinger and thumb.

"Twenty-two."

"Twenty-two!" he exclaimed in amazement. Then a sudden fit of childish anger swept over him, but accompanied – seeing the scope it offered him for oratory – by an exultation tantamount, almost, to a brimming over of love. Fervently then: "Ah, only twenty-two meagre autumns, winters, summers, springs? What do you know of it, to make you want to throw in the sponge so soon? What have you known yet of the music of the world? Of light and dark, of sea and sky? Of the wind? The moon? Or of mankind, the belovèd strangers you brush shoulders with, each of them bearing in his heart rich hopes, ripe sorrows?. . . Have you ever asked yourself what myriads of men and women from time immemorial have hoped and despaired before you? Billions upon billions, their name is Legion. Imagine them here, thronging Villa Bellini, thronging the plain of Catania, and this whole island, the whole world, jam-packed tight. Here at Acquicella, at Cibari, at Novalucello; but there too, in Lisbon, Cincinnati, Vladivostok; all like sardines, jam-packed on the terraces, the rooftops, a sea of small black dots, of raised arms, raised faces, as at the Day of Judgement, arms raised up like the shafts of empty carts. . ."

Ages now since he had taught in class. His voice let him down, ruptured into a fit of coughing that seemed unlikely ever to stop. Naomi waited patiently, watching him with listless, sceptical eyes. On the bench, on top of his book, she had dumped her handbag, half-open and revealing the box of syringes, the dosed-out packets: a death-machine too modern for him to recognize as such. And she just watched him, waiting for a respite in his coughing.

He too wished for nothing better, eager as he was to pick up where he had left off. For though his eloquence admittedly stemmed in small part from savouring his erstwhile bent for rhetoric, it arose far more from a fullness of heart, a commingling of rage and pity. A humble, envious, compassionate rage for so many young lives thrown away in the highways and byways of the world, and the days of youth cast to the winds. . . To the mortifying vexation of those whose own days are numbered.

"Have you any idea," he began again more quietly, "how many stars are in the sky? How many constellations, from Andromeda to Virgo? Well, then, the number of the dead is greater still. And all of them, could they but come alive again for an instant, jam-packed there in the plain, you'd see them raise their arms to heaven, crying, begging for a mite of sound and of light, at the price of any tortures or agonies whatsoever. For torture there is not, that they would be unwilling to undergo in exchange for a pitiful fistful of light, just one single measly second of light. . . All, all of them would raise their hands to heaven, if they could. But they cannot. Because they are nothing but dust, nothing but dust. . ."

The girl started to laugh, in short bursts like a car refusing to start.

"That's a good one, I must say! But you've forgotten something. What becomes of all the dust, then? Why, by now there ought to be so much, such great mountains of it, that the whole world would be smothered with it. So you just tell me, why doesn't the world grow bigger?"

He had worn himself out, closed his eyes again as he rummaged blindly through his pockets. He found a little phial, took out a pill, placed it under his tongue. Then, wearily: "It grows all right. It grows. Even if nobody notices it yet. But one of

119

these days the seas and the river will silt up with the ashes of the dead, and the earth will perish."

In the silence that followed the voice of the ice-cream man sounded distant, dispirited: "Come on now, kiddies, squeeze out a tear and mum'll buy yer one!"

Gaetano was alone in taking this in, and made eye-signs at the girl, grabbed her hand and hauled her off towards the box on wheels still concealed around the corner.

"Grand-dad, hang on a mo'. Don't go," the girl called to the old man without looking round.

Second Day

He didn't hang on for them. The cold nipped at him and he felt the need for his arm-chair at home, a glass of wine. But next day, at the same time, despite a threat of rain, a zealous impulse drew him to the usual old bench as if he had made an unspoken promise. A few minutes later there the two of them were, when the rain had already begun and the old man was scarcely to be seen under the dome of his umbrella, stern and stony beneath the weight of his overcoat.

"So how's the trouble?" he enquired, touching the girl's forehead with a finger.

But back she came at him with "No, Mr Teacher, no. I'm not going to tell you the story of my life. You don't know the lingo. You're much too old, and speak funny, and wear specs and have this book no one can understand. . ."

She took the book from him, opened it at random, stabbed her finger at a random line. "Maybe this book can help me. Maybe the answer's here where my finger is. Maybe it says here what someone who doesn't know what to do ought to do. But I don't know Greek. And your eyes have gone phut. . ."

The old man took her hand a moment, gently stroked the bandaged wrist, questioned her with his eyes and got a nod of affirmation.

"Ah, so that's why you're so pale. . ." And he hugged her in beside him under the umbrella, helped the boy to climb on to his knee. The boy remained happily silent – nothing he liked better than to listen in on two grown-ups nattering.

"We don't talk the same language, you and me," she went on, "but I bet you can rustle up a fairy-story for Tano here. Or rather, for us both. . ."

"Would a dream do you?"

The boy protested. "No, I want a really truly fairy-story! A new one, please. I've known all the old ones for years and years."

"Very well. Let us say, then, that once upon a time there was a prince who lost his way in a wood. Now, in this wood there was a castle. In he goes and there he finds a ladder all made of silver, a magic ladder: put a foot on an upward rung and you are a whole year older; step down and you lose a year. So our prince. . ."

The pause was planned but the girl did not fall for it. Tano did though: "What did the prince do?"

"What would *you* have done?" asked the old man and the girl with one voice. And laughed when first Tano cried, "Climb up! Grow big!", then, quickly taking it back, "No! Wait! Climb down, climb down!"

"You see, little one, you can't make up your mind. And neither could the prince. He hung there on one rung and didn't know what to do. And there he would be to this day but for. . ."

"But for what?"

"But for a giant who arrived on the scene. And this giant had not a boot to his name! He needed a size ninety-nine, *he* did."

"So then?"

"So he came to the castle. One day he had seen a couple of enormous bathtubs there, and he very much hoped they might fit him. . ."

121

He broke off. The young man of the day before was standing before them. Hatless, hair on end and dripping with rain, a wet but winsome figure. A stocky fellow – with his leather garb and handsome scowl you couldn't tell whether he was student or truck-driver.

Naomi raised her head sharply. "What's it this time?"

"This time it's that you're coming with me, right back home."

He grabbed her arm, pulled her to her feet, but she fought back, while Tano with his little fists punched at the fellow's legs. Even the old man got up, snapped shut his umbrella and brandished it menacingly. "You brute," he cried. "Get out of here!"

At this the young man unexpectedly released his grip and burst into tears. "It's all you!" he sobbed accusingly at Naomi. "You, you, you!" And he blubbed on. Then he shook himself: "Come home!" he cried one last time, and walked away alone.

And the little boy, also crying by this time, "But *laces*, what does the giant do for *laces*?" he asked through his tears.

In the scuffle the book had landed up in the mud. Naomi retrieved it and wiped it clean. Plainly she was not going to comment on what had occurred. Her voice was expressionless. "D'you get the stories you tell from this book?" she asked.

"Oh no, I just make them up." The old man followed her lead, behaving as if nothing had happened. "Telling lies is the only hobby left to me now."

"I *thought* as much," said the girl. "Your eyes are bloodshot, and that's the sign of a fibber! All the same, I can't deny it, I wouldn't have minded you being my teacher at school, and me reading this book with you. What's it about, Mr Teacher?"

The old man stroked the book with his fingertips. "It's the story of an old man leaning on a girl's arm." And, without glancing down at it, he recited:

"O Antigone, thou daughter of a blind old man, where are

we come to now? Is this the open country or a city of men? And what city might it be? Will there be anyone, even today, to greet with gifts, be they never so poor, this homeless Oedipus?"

The rain meanwhile had ceased. Indeed the sun had come out, shimmering on the heads of the busts and rapidly drying the fallen leaves in the avenue.

"But what about the *laces*?" insisted the boy.

"Oh," said the old man, "no need for them. Those were very special shoes, porcelain moccasins..." Then, to the girl: "But what do you do? How do you make a living? Taking children for walks?"

"When I can get the job. I'm really a welfare worker, but I don't get much welfare done. I'm the one that needs the doing good to."

From somewhere in the background came the hullaballoo of a roundabout. There must be a funfair not far off, which the return of the sunshine had spurred into renewed activity.

"Have *you* got a daughter, then? Someone to lean on the arm of?"

"No," he answered, "I am alone in the world. I have adopted as my only child the ghost of myself when young."

"A ghost won't give you much of a hand the day you need laying out."

"So far as that goes, one dies better alone. It's the carnival of the lonely soul, is death."

"Carnival? But I thought you were telling me yesterday that *living* was one long carnival..."

"One day you'll understand that every truth has a contrary that is also true. Like the mack you're wearing – reversible..."

They fell silent. Yesterday's ice-cream man recommended his rigmarole, but Gaetano seemed oblivious to him. He was listening all agog to the grown-ups.

"I don't much fancy that young fellow," the old man said.

He had not expected her to give in so suddenly, or that she

would so suddenly consent to unburden herself of her secret, like a woman giving birth.

"Me though, I've fancied him since I was fifteen, and he's fancied me. He's been lusting for me and me for him."

"Is *that* all?" The old man shrugged. "Why, what's so terrible about loving a man and being loved in return?"

"What's terrible," she burst out, "is that I'm doomed. The choice I've got isn't between passion and common sense, it's between two dooms, two disasters: to go back to him and die of it or to leave him and die of that."

She hesitated, then, as if spelling it out: "You see, there are three of us. We are orphans and live together, him, me, and my sister. It was him, my own brother, who corrupted us both from the start, when we were still kids. And now my sister is stuck in a wheel-chair. Her kidneys are a mishmash and she's raving mad. Every night she says to me, 'Little sister, go to him, sleep with him tonight. Love for me, scream for me. All I want is to hear you both from here in my room.'"

"It's a rare case," said the old man. "But no more shocking than many one reads about in the papers."

"That's all very well, but what am I to *do*? I left home and went out nursemaiding, you see, but I'll never hold out. And him, look how he dogs me, never gives me a moment's peace! I'm as scared of him as I am of rats! But he only has to touch me and I go weak at the knees, burn all over and can't say no."

She got up. "And that's not all, grand-dad. I've a bigger killer than that up my sleeve I haven't told you about. But I'll tell you tomorrow."

She picked up her bag, took the boy by the hand. His face now wore all the gravity of a grown-up, was irresolute, unhappy. She started to leave, but after a step or two turned back.

"What've you got to tell me about God then, grand-dad? That he exists?"

He got up in his turn and slowly joined her.

"What a question to ask! Very probably he does, but we can't see him clearly any longer. Only fragments, filaments, flotsam and jetsam, a whisper here and there in a ray of moonlight on a windowsill, a breath among shady mulberry leaves, the lament of a girl who wants to do herself in. . . Come now, I'll explain better tomorrow. I'll have to think about it. . ."

"See you tomorrow then. Same time?"

"Unfailingly."

Third Day

Villa Bellini, in the early part of the morning, could almost be taken for private gardens. A gardener in slate-grey overalls bending over a flower-bed, planting out the date in flowers – January 20th or thereabouts. Old-age pensioners coming and going. A middle-aged governess, tall and gaunt, letting herself be led by the hand towards "Celebrities' Walk" by a small boy who seems in a hurry.

On their way up Tano asks, "What size shoes d'you take?" but he gets no answer. "Giants wear number ninety-nine," he goes on. Then, "I don't even know your name yet."

"Vincenza," the woman tells him.

"Naomi was a nicer name," murmurs the boy.

Now he has tugged his hand out of hers and is chasing his ball tossed far, far ahead to where a man is sitting on a bench, his face invisible behind an open newspaper. Tano plays at rolling the ball between the man's feet, and laughs in anticipation. But he stops like a shot when a strange face appears from behind the paper screen, the face of an old man he has never seen before, who hands back the ball without a word and goes back to his reading.

A little later a stocky young man appears at the top of the avenue, again in his leather outfit. He recognizes the boy from

afar, his eyes search for someone near him but see only a middle-
aged woman, tall and gaunt, the *signorina* from the kinder-
garten, Vincenza Sbezzi.

He takes a seat on the bench opposite and drags at a cigarette.
The boy doesn't notice him: he is scrutinizing the old man
behind the paper. Finally he tosses back his blond quiff, bounces
his ball three times, pins it to the ground with his foot, then
stretches out prone and gazes at it there, inert and dead, pressing
his palms to his temples and talking very softly to himself.

The Keeper of Ruins

CALL IT COINCIDENCE, call it vocation, but I've done next to nothing all my life but watch over things dead or dying. Now that I'm getting on in years, and can look back from an eminence near the summit, I never cease to be struck, among the random zigzags and paradoxes of my journey, by this persistent thread which gives them, or at least seems to give them, the lie. Maybe it is true that each man carries loyalty to a certain voice inherent in his very blood, and that he cannot but obey that voice, however many defections occasion may incite him to. Thus destiny appears to have assigned me to perpetual sentry-duty, to be keeper not of laws or of treasure-hoards but of tombs and ruins; if not, indeed, of nobody and of nothing...

I remember that as a child, whenever we played cops and robbers, all the cops and all the robbers immediately agreed to cast me in the role of "It". All very well, had they not been equally unanimous, once I was hiding my eyes, in dropping hostilities and sauntering off, leaving me all innocent around the corner, ears astrain for non-existent enemies.

Later, one wartime Christmas night, it fell to my lot to stamp my feet for cold on picket duty outside an ammunition dump – empty and disused for years as I learnt next morning from the corporal who came to relieve me. What quaint military philosophy, to demand obedience to an heroic code even when its *raison d'être* is dead and buried... I (having been through high school) thought of Catherine the Great's famous sentry, destined never to leave his rickety sentry-box, and I persuaded

127

myself that his fate was an emblem for me, maybe for all of us. . .

But to my tale. I'll mention two other periods in my life, not imposed on me by others, but sought out and chosen by me: the time I was caretaker of a graveyard; and when I was keeper of a lighthouse. The first was a task more cheerful and health-giving than you might suppose, with that smooth enamelled green on fine sunny days, and the peaceful tedium of it, the tiny lizardess cheekily peeking through a crack in a tombstone and the marble angel signposting heaven with three remaining fingers. . .

A village graveyard this, with visitors once in a blue moon tethering their mules to the gate like wild-western gunslingers hitching their horses to a post, then making for some tombstone, categorical and glum, their arms encumbered with chrysanthemums. On leaving they would hand me a tip – fruit and vegetables – and exort me to change the water in the vases and keep the grass trim. Little did they know that every evening I had sweeter dealings with those shades, and that (better far than all these insipid wreaths) I would console them with an impromptu recital on the mandolin.

It didn't last. Migliavacca's *Mazurka* seemed a blasphemy to Rinzivillo the road-mender, as he squatted down beyond the wall on business of his own, no less perturbed than disturbed by the plucking of my strings. I was denounced, surprised *in flagrante delicto* of sound, forgiven, caught at it again. . . I got the sack, I took my leave. But not before I had rejoiced the dead, grave by grave, with one last serenade.

I had better luck with the lighthouse. If I left in the end it was of my own free will and the urge for change. Needless to say it was a derelict lighthouse, built long since at the expense of a fishermen's co-operative to pinpoint the coast with the intermittent flash of its lantern; a useless lighthouse now, since in those waters not a smack put to sea and the last fisherman was dead. Not even the steamers passing far offshore, opulent with radar and similar devilries, could now require our morsel of light, our paltry Tom Thumb's crumbs. . . So I set myself up there by general consent, and made myself master of the place, on condition that I give the machinery an occasional run to prevent it rusting, and keep the windows shipshape, and tickle the trippers on Bank Holiday nights by sullying the moonlight with the bi-chromatic hide-and-seek of my great gyrating lantern. In the summer I enjoyed this assignment as small-time pyrotechnist, nor did I crave any other contact with my fellow men than this: to look down from my eyrie on all their sheep-like meekness and count their heads from the porthole of my quarters, all high and mighty inside my lantern, unique and out of reach. . .

Winter was another story. With beaches deserted and houses shuttered up, I devised myself histrionic pastimes. Swathed in my Man-of-Aran oilskins I'd go out of an evening on to the circular gallery, torch in hand to cleave out warnings of an imaginary cyclone or still more imaginary shipwreck. Or else (and more frequently) I would write lines to declaim before the mirror:

> As the perfidious keeper of a lighthouse
> I lure the boats that seek me on to the rocks
> And snigger to myself, and rub my hands. . .

O yes, I wrote these words and more besides, and what d'you think came of it? A customs officer confiscated my notebook when he came snooping round, convinced that from my vantage point I was tipping the wink to the smugglers' motorboats. He turned the place upside down, for those lines, the long and the short of them, looked to him like the code of some wireless telegraph; in those black and white marks he descried the esoteric *corpus delicti* of a very palpable crime. He was only half wrong.

*　　*　　*

You find me today ensconced in my ultimate stronghold: a car-wrecker's yard. Here I am monarch and God Almighty on the best of all possible thrones. I even earn something. People come from all over to bring me, gratis, the wreckage of every car-crash, with the blood of the slain still wet on the mudguards. Others come searching for odd bits and pieces, spares unobtainable elsewhere, buried in the scrap-heap: a door, a baffle, a deflector... I am happy. Far more so than that Greek sentry of old (remember?) on the roof of Agamemnon's palace, crouched on his elbows like a dog, probing the assemblies of the stars and the secrets of their rising and setting... Ah no, at my side – unlike his – there stalks no fear. I still have my mandolin and if I sing it is not to banish ghosts but to summon them.

Happy: there's no other word for it. Here is the haven towards which, groping, I have moved; here I find a meaning for the race I have run, if it has been a race; for my flight, if it has been a flight.

How do I stay alive? Being moderate by nature, that's no problem. I have a small hut to sleep in. A minibus (minus the seats) does me for kitchen, pantry and dining-room. On a gas-ring I cook Spartan fare, and consume it with mock ceremonial, Grand Hotel style, playing waiter and diner in turn. A little act for which I solemnly award myself cheers or jeers before retiring to my sleeping quarters with a humdrum pack of cards to sample the delights of solitaire. I know every kind there is, but I love to think up new ones, the better to grapple with the radiant sequences of suits from Ace to King and the baffling surprises of the odd man out. And if I lose more often than I win, that merely doubles the metaphysical ecstasy of daring to wager against the vainglory of God. In any case, what is more sedative, more sleep-inveigling, than nursing the hope of getting one's own back?

As for chit-chat, I never indulge in it with a living soul, bar a yes or no to customers and a few quips to the driver of the breakdown lorry, who delivers my stock-in-trade every Monday.

For all other needs I exploit every mechanical and chemical resource my quarry of old iron and sheet-metal has to offer. In the cold winter months, for instance, I burn leftover oil from some dismantled engine; in the height of summer I run a radiator fan off a battery. Lighting? From a generator. Water? From a big truck-tank hoisted above the roof. I shave with an old cut-throat razor with the aid of a rearview mirror; for my afternoon nap I seek out the reclining seat of an elderly Lancia Flaminia; the hour of noon I sound for myself on a car-horn.

You'll say it's a Robinson Crusoe kind of life, and so be it. Even though I live smack beside the motorway, and see the live cars hurtling monstrously past no more than a hundred yards away. But I'm certainly not short of space. The clearing I camp in is State property, a plot of land expropriated to give elbow-room to the earth-moving operations. The debris of loose earth, brown or chalky, bulldozed at that time on to the grass, has little by little killed it. Pounded by countless feet and wheels, the soil has forgotten the seasons of sap and of seed-time, con-serving a scant relict of them only in three trees in a row, like three stubborn caryatids remaining upright after the collapse of the architrave.

They it is, in my design for a city, that represent The Garden. I am, you see, pursuing a project, that of tracing the geometry of a city with the skeletons of motorcars. Not, therefore, scattering them haphazardly in the first vacant space, but arranging them in order and in line, their skulls aimed in the appointed direc-tion, to create a semblance of buildings bordering a High Street or ringing a Circus. In my dream town I already have a gridiron of zones, according to the precepts of Hippodamus, with streets ready christened: Blue Simca Street, Three Renaults Boulevard, Lame Alfa Alley (No Thoroughfare)... A main square is coming into being, encompassed around with black limousines; in the centre, convoluted, for all the world like an equestrian tumour, is the carcass of a bus which impact warped and fire blackened

131

with leprous burns. Thus, unconsciously, with these aligned and lidded sepulchres, I have been creating a replica of the country graveyard of my youth. So much so that, come All Souls' Day, I would not be surprised to see the former proprietors of each vehicle return to revisit it bearing flowers, and to hear Rinzivillo bawl me out once more from beyond the wall, before squatting down to his business...

No one comes, of course; but all the same, as I pace at cock-crow between scrap-metal hedges, I try to imagine in each interior the forms of life which one time hovered there. I hearken to amorous whispers, words of wrath, fevered or fatuous stirrings of the heart. A people of the dead roams my domain from end to end, an invisible flock that dotes on me and which I feed as the spirit moves me. Not without special regard for the showpieces: the Mercedes of a murder victim, its windscreen milky from bulletry; a massive hearse behind which it is hard not to conjure up a cortège, crêpe and muffled drums, black-masked horses, black-plumed cuirassiers...

I have particular esteem for these specimens, and never fail to bid them a fond goodnight. "Nine o'clock and all's well," I murmur, and almost feel I am putting them to bed and tucking in the blankets.

Think what you may I am not a madman, nor yet a novice in life. Who can say it is I who am wrong, not you, if I am content with my harvest of ashes, and glory only in history dead and done for, in the allurements of dereliction? In truth there is nothing in the world outside but to me is foreign or hostile: I have nothing to do with it, I don't understand it. Even of the woman who visits me occasionally from the Autogrill I ask no news of peace or war; I get the thing done with brief, technical gestures, send her packing, and become once more the voluptuary of solitude...

Put to the test of old age, what will become of me? When, like a noble river at the estuary, I silt up, and am myself reduced to a catastrophe to be cared for?

The future holds no fears for me. Whatever end awaits me it is sure that elsewhere, after death, I shall have to mount guard once more. I know, but will not tell you, over which absence or impotence or ruin.

The Joyous Adventures of
the Punished Child

THEY LOCKED HIM IN the lumber-room for some trifling misdeed.

The first thing he does is bolt the door himself, from the inside. He has no intention of running the risk of some last-minute forgiveness, some unwished-for amnesty. Let them – the others – stay outside in disgrace, excluded from his life, his prisoners without knowing it.

He bolts the door behind him then, and a mighty jubilation quickens his blood; solitude goes to his head. He is free at last, monarch of all he surveys, sovereign of a country with no confines; one which, though familiar to him, changes none the less at every moment, like the waves and the clouds, which as you watch are time and again made new.

He will explore it inch by inch, with all the circumspection of a scouting-party, make a census of its population of scrapped furniture and fittings, discarded playthings, funny costumes in store for fancy-dress parties to come. His project, if a vague impulse can be called a project, is to transfigure this trash-heap of memories into a fairground of marvels.

Spellbound he gazes at the sailing-ship in its bottle. A miniature three-master, crimson painted, with her name – *Maris Stella* – in black on her prow, complete with sails and rigging from stem to stern, sound enough still to lie at anchor or haul to windward, had she not run aground on this glass shoal after long warfare with the winds. . . The boy tries the narrow bottleneck with his finger, compares it in puzzlement with the size of the vessel, and feels his imagination slip like sand through his fingers.

Next it's the old mirror's turn to disconcert him, as he stands before it and ponders on his reflection. The oval, foxed with brown, in its vineleaf-pattern frame, offers him a lacklustre medley of colours, the light blue of his smock, the pallor of his forehead, the red glow of his lips. And a pair of eyes surprised by themselves, now-you-see-them-now-you-don't, in a batting of eyelids.

"Me," says the child, and touches himself, starts to touch himself all over, rebaptize himself. "Forehead," he says. "Eyes," he smiles. "Nose," he laughs. Before even tiring of the game he throws a piece of chintz over the mirror and, by blotting it out, feels he has killed himself.

What will he do now? Whither will he be led by the delectable vagary of his steps?

His first journey is to his father's chest, left just as it was when he went away. The child plunges in a hand at random, comes up with the big print of the caves of Postumia, with the minuscule tourist wandering among the stalagmites, in his hand a miner's lamp.

He leafs through the same old books, *With Iron and Fire, The Secret Silver Mine, The Poet's Mystery*. . . He dallies over another, tempted. He knows he is forbidden to open it, but he holds the closed volume in both hands, stroking the cover. . .

A sudden whim summons him elsewhere. On he goes. On the floor, its flaps folded like wings, is the collage-screen of newspaper clippings that used to be in his sister's room. He stands it upright with some effort, opens it and hides behind it, scarcely knowing from whom. Through a rent in the paper his eye searches in vain for some non-existent prey or persecutor.

He is not discouraged: for as long as he remembers he has had a fancy for spying. He thinks of one summer, at the country house near the river, and the noonday silence under the mulberry-tree thronged with birds. And not even they made a sound, stunned with heat as they were. Later, late in the evening, raising himself on his elbow from the pillow, he listened in to his father and mother's chatter in the next-door room. His father was bragging about him, speaking of a queenly bride one day, and of farmlands rich in spring-water, and immense fortune and wisdom and good health to come... His mother replied yes, yes, and she would go walking out on Easter Day arm in arm with her daughter-in-law the queen, and everyone would turn and gape...

Look now, here is the telescope, a gift once treasured, now abandoned. He adjusts it to his eye, focuses it; but near-by objectives do not satisfy him. He clambers up on a chair to get a view over the edge of the skylight. The eyepiece reveals an almost twilight sky; down there is the plain, with a white horse grazing in a meadow; close below, the town, its roofs, its chimneys, the tranquil gesture of the church-towers towards the rising moon. How huge is a church-tower when you look through the one end; and how wee when you turn the telescope round. A strange and wonderful thing, that nothing in the world stays always the same size; that everything can shrink and grow as you please, according to which way round you hold a telescope. Strange and wonderful too, that a schooner can pass through the neck of a bottle... Heaven knows how big a hand must seem to a fly, when poised to squash it on a windowsill; and how vast to an ant the shadow of a menacing shoe...

The child feels old in a world that cannot be measured, a dumb show of shapes and of ages that lengthen and shorten for no reason, in which grown-ups and children do nothing but swap over ages and roles. And they all will die in the end, dressed in black, just as his father died, a year ago.

He feels old, does the child, yet wonderstruck and glad to be alive. His eye is caught by a dark blob on the whitewash: a spider benumbed and killed by some long-past frost, it crumbles beneath his thumb. From a half-open drawer he is enticed by a pack of Neapolitan cards; he chooses two of them and weds them into the golden trophy of a *settebello*. Discarded in a stove-in bucket he discovers a length of well-rope, and plays for a moment at hanging himself. But the noose comes merrily to bits in his hand. He plays at blindman's buff with a hanky, pictures himself as master of flying carpets, bosun of floating islands, a diver diving for philosophers' stones...

What is he weaving for himself, a romance or a challenge? He knows not which.

He moves back to the mirror, uncovers it, leans it up where the light is better. With rapid hands he undresses, dropping his clothes in a circle round sockless feet, and stands naked, skinny, defenceless, before the glass. Looking at himself, touching himself, rebaptizing himself yet again. Serious, this time, with a frown of bold resolve. He palps his shoulder blades, counts the ribs in his meagre chest, fingertip-questions the pale small buds of his nipples, the dry hollow of his belly, the mysterious navel. With surprise and trepidation his hand scurries to discover the sleepy little snake between his legs, the rose of the glans in bud...

Who could it be, save himself, to have drawn back the bolt? O how else can have entered these troupes of jugglers, of fiddlers, of sorcerer kings? Salamanders crackle in a blazing brazier, foamy curls hang on the crest of a wave, then spill, swirl down into the depths. The lark that of late took wing is no more to be seen...

Now seven maidens of Sheba come bringing him the Great Bear. With them is Harlequin on mule-back, and guitars, and conches, and a wafting fan...

Eventually his mother came and called outside the door.

The Beauty of the Universe

IT WAS ON THE SEAT of a swing, and on his forty-sixth birthday, that Severino Paceco became aware of the beauty of the universe. He had risen betimes, in the patrician country mansion where he was in service as preceptor, and while he was leisurely pacing the garden, awaiting the gong for breakfast, he happened to notice, with genuine surprise, the brand-new swing which Don Gualtiero, master of the house, had had attached by twin ropes to a bough, and which was swaying in the breeze.

Never had he made trial of any vehicle so elusive, nor for that matter, even as a child, had he taken pleasure in venturing on seesaws and roundabouts; still less, with string in hand, in racing over the countryside partaking of the caprices of a kite. Severino was a man of contemplative, indoor disposition, redolent of ink and blotting paper, whose limbs seemed as natively wedded to a desk as to a throne are those of a king. Nevertheless, on this occasion the swing contrived to tempt him: tremulant, beckoning, a tiny mare on heat for a gallop. No sooner thought than done: he approached it, tested with a finger the sides of the "chair-volant", gave it a push to make it swing the further. The diffident look he cast around him revealed no presence, no sign of life, save only the motionless dot of a sea-going vessel on the horizon and, nearer at hand, a harmless peacock emerging from behind the house in all its fantailed vainglory. Nothing more did it need, for him to doff his three-cornered hat, tuck in the tails of his coat and, with such verve as he would never have credited, leap on to the machine to swing.

It was August. Bluebottles, for all the world like pinguid hornets, were buzzing all round him. And Severino laughed aloud and alone.

Now up now down the swing conveyed him. He had grasped the ropes tightly, as if they were the reins in some breakneck horserace or the knotted sheets of an escaping prisoner. But while, painfully skinning his palms and at the risk of a spill, he was imparting with his body an ever more temerarious motion to the swing-seat – though not failing thereby to plunder earth and sky for the very utmost his sight could encompass – his blood, bewildered by these unaccustomed high jinks, rushed to his head and persuaded him to seek a truce. It was at this point, when the little cockleshell had slowed to a more sober tempo, that of a cradle or a hammock, that Severino began to fall prey to a sudden abandon, and was confusedly stirred by the beauty of all that is. Nor did this sentiment remain placid and dormant within him, but in the manner of wine-must fermenting in the vat, bubbled to his lips in frothy tides of sound, and issued forth in a copious hosanna and hymn.

"O sky, O firmament!" he struck up therefore in ear-smiting tones. "Beauteous thou art, most beauteous. Thyself and thy clouds, of which no man can tell what images they be, nor yet of what: whether ciphers hieroglyphic and pedagogical, or the debris of lofty castles, or reviews of kingly fleets, or cavalcades of dreams... Until one morn, as it might be today, a wind undoeth them, the heat melteth them away, and thou of a sudden art this clear rock crystal, this hard orb of azure, the pupil of a one-eyed, all-things-seeing god..." With a soft puff he blew away a fleck of scurf fallen on his shoulder, and thus proceeded: "How fain would I, unfathomable firmament, be thy sentinel all the days that remain to me! Atop some watch-tower, a beaker of water and crust of bread my only company, for to learn if thou art flawless emerald or gibbous pearl, the entrails of all or the maw of nothingness... Wherefore some there be who declare thou hast no confines, others that thou dost arch and circle round to set thy teeth in thine own flaming tail... And thou goest yoking together suns and moons, and weaving dawns and sunsets, and darting forth lightning zigzag among the fronds of the galaxies... Serpent-firmament! Arboreal firmament! Mysterious, perfect, immeasurably beauteous firmament!"

He was unaware, was Severino, that a girl had crept up stealthily through the trees and was spying on him, albeit with eyes still bleared with sleep. Barefoot, clad in a skimpy petticoat that revealed a great deal of leg, but surmounted, and of a colour less blond than yellow, by the prodigious wheatsheaf of her hair. A girl by the name of Rosina, ward in the house of her patrician uncle, and grown up there, wild and idle, despite the zeal with which the latter attempted to raise her with greater industry than if she had been his own daughter. Appointed (after a host of others) to make a lady of her, Severino, famous in the neighbourhood for learning and authoritativeness, had succeeded no better than the rest in capturing the attention of his pupil. So little, in fact, that the least trifle sufficed to steal her heart away, be it flash of sunlight on the windowpanes, scent of orange-flower water in a pot, or *do re mi* of a distant spinet...

He had a fine job of it, lecturing about "accidents" and "quiddities", conjugating nasal inchoative verbs, and, when in desperate straits, relating some ancient fable. Not without agitation, whenever one or another lewdness on the part of Jove provoked interpellations which put him on hot coals; and dumbfounded, above all, by the alien knee that boldly sought his own beneath the table. For Rosina had made it a point of honour to stir up – if any such vestige remained in those winter quarters – the embers of his sensuality. Simply to catch the professor hopping, so to speak, while herself remaining sheltered by that aplomb of indifference to which she had recourse in her moments of greatest daring, raising a single supercilious eyebrow and, with the tapering nail of her little finger, twisting a lock of the wheaten gold that struck upon her cheek.

141

There she was, then, this early-morning girl, crouched among the box-bushes, listening all ears (at last) to the words of Severino; at first with instinctive womanish inquisitiveness, purposing as ever to poke fun at the pedant; then seized with amazement, and not only amazement but inexplicable joy, at hearing so many abstruse and alluring sublimities. As for Paceco, he was already so far extended – and with such afflatus of unprecedented spirits – in the catalogue and panegyric of the entire created world, that he did not observe her, but gave fresh though erratic impetus to his acrobatics, now varying from *adagio* to *con brio*, now dwindling down to metronomic monotony. In such a manner that from among the foliage his upsweeps and downswoops appeared to supply the bass to the melody of his words. Unless it be that the contrary were true: that it was eloquence that accompanied and commented on his motion.

"Thou, O sea!" Thus he resumed his oration. And unable to do so with his hands tight grasping the ropes, with a tilt of his chin he indicated the line of blue beyond the hedge. "Thou, O sea, innumerable-tonguèd sea, that consentest to lap the humblest recesses in the rocks no less than the most amplitudin-ous gulfs of the continents; now ebbing and flowing, mild and enticing, now roaring with all the conch-horns and trumpets of the world's last day. Great dome of moist cool shade on the drowned man's brow, complaisant womb for the daring swim-mer to enter... O sea, what can I tell thee, but that wild thou bewitchest and tender thou enamourest me? And that each and every time I look upon thee, naught more perfectly than thy being, and being not, and coming into being again, is like unto the nature of God?..."

Who knows what further he might not have spoken, of fire and the earth, of the minerals, the plants and the animals that dwell therein, of the seasons that clothe and unclothe it... and of the grandeur of man, and his sense of taste, of scent, of hearing, of touch; and of his sight above all, to discern the scattered marvels hidden in the heart of the light. And how man laughs and weeps, sleeps and wakes. And remembers, remembers... Severino would have told over all the feelings ever felt by man, countless and stupendous in their aureate alchemies. He would have spoken of the crystals and the corals, of lava and of water, and how rust stains a fallen leaf and a bud quivers on an apple-tree; and of the scent of mown hay after rain. Of the precious gems, the mountain ranges, the tread of elephants and the flutter of moths; and of time, of beauty, of death... And who knows what more he would not have praised and hosanna'd, this Severino, if (emerging from the bushes, in the manner of one who recklessly confronts a mettlesome quadruped) the girl had not planted herself before him, seizing her chance to reduce the oscillations of the swing, and finally to bring it to a standstill. Succeeding in this, yes, but not without the poor fool landing up in her arms, lock, stock and barrel, and in a *mélange* of rumpled linen and aromas of youthful breath and the warmth of flesh but lately arisen from bed. The unfortunate defended himself as best he might, panting as he was from his recent exertions but, worse still, burning from the childishness in which he had been caught red-handed by the girl; from her very proximity, too, as she leant upon him, suddenly dumbstruck and apparently stunned. Her bare feet deep in dew, her flimsy night-veils all in disarray, Rosina stood clinging to him, shielding him a little to eastward. Whence now the sun, already risen, but tarrying with the wariness of a conspirator behind the crest of a hill, at that instant unmasked and scattered himself, like a spattering egg-yolk, to every point of the compass, sensationally drenching all things great and small there present in the plain. And amongst these, her hair.

It is reasonable to suppose that this, for Severino, was the first kiss of his life. Nor, at first, was the taste of it such as to please him a great deal, he being as inept as she in dodging reciprocal noscs and finding the proper way of sealing lip to lip. And it may be he would have drawn back with the flush on his cheek, as much in disappointment as in panic, had not Rosina forcibly dislodged him from his swing-saddle and contrived that they should fall together into the grass. To what purpose they knew neither one nor t'other, save that from the girl to the man there seemed to pass an electric charge, that made brisk passage through his veins; thereupon, not otherwise than in a duel of echoes, to strike back at her, redoubled and fiery; teaching the pair of them an unheralded dexterity of movement, feverish in the releasing of buttons from button-holes, in the loosing and losing of garments until, no less colossal than clumsy, he was looming above her and fell upon her limbs and within them.

O woe and alas little butterfly flighty Rosina! Where now are the delicate combs for your hair, and where is the girdle that girt you about, and what storm-cloud bears you away? What undoing is this that bedims your eyes while a serpent of dolorous delight grows slowly within you, there beneath the canopy of leaves where you tumble together? A rich, rich death is this dying of yours and dying again into life, this perverse delice of conquering for naught but once more to succumb! In vain does the light strike your nape with a nosegay of flowers, and time twixt your lashes is a sand-hill that sifts softly softly away. . .

But Severino, how fares Severino? Trodden by mysterious hoofs, he seems to be traversing some deep place underground and endless; and thence, from his buried Elysium, to hear birds winging in to throng his temples, their cries borne away on the wind like a far-away view-halloo. He knows now what was wanting to his inventory of the beauties of the world: the honey of a breath of Eve to mingle with his, and beneath his touch the soft white bread of her breasts, and a grotto within her wherein to make themselves one, with the selfsame unanimous heartbeat, on the selfsame bride-bed of shadows. . .

This now he knows; and he knows also that henceforth all will be clearer to him, more tranquil withal, more. . .

*   *   *

They heard not the gong that summoned them; nor, thereafter, the servants' voices, the baying of bloodhounds on the scent; nor the echo of footsteps round the great chestnut. They did not observe Don Gualtiero with his left hand part the leafy screen, and in his right a sword.

The Old Man and the Tree

THAT JUNE SEEMED TO HIM at first no different from the others, the many others, of his life, but the old man soon realized that this was an artificial, an alien month, the bearer of mysterious and baleful sentiments. It would not be easy to make friends with it. It is never easy to be on friendly terms with the seasons, it always seems they are going against the grain, and that their phases of equanimity and frenzy do their level best to contradict our own: those, I mean, of our own feelings and thoughts. Above all if you are old, and live alone out in the country, in a house too big for you, and have nobody to talk to except that everlasting solitary lizard. Then you are at the mercy of the bullying of the seasons, your bargain with time breaks down like a stone soaked in vinegar and salt...

So the old man felt of a sudden weary at heart, a heart over eighty years old; and too restless to stay in the house, he slung his gun over his shoulder and went out walking through the fields.

What exactly he would do he had no idea. It was as if they had bound his head about with thorns. He looked up at the sun: an ersatz red it was, straight from the dyer's, oozing with putrid juices, septic blood. The very birds seemed in fear of it, hidden on the ground, in the grass, far from the sky. Beyond the vineyard the river, overhung with bastard, barren vine-creepers fringing the escarpment, had shrunk to no more than a trickle between two ranks of spindly canes. A short hop would have sufficed to carry him across, but he did not make it. It more suited his fancy to stoop down over a puddle – one of many – in which water lay languid among pebbles and gravel.

He saw, he made out, a face. It was not his face, he erased it with a boot, there was no reason to believe in it; it was the face of a traitor. He paused on this word, indicted himself, acquitted himself: it was not he who had played traitor, but the years. They it was who had travestied that face, burdening it with bumps and furrows. How many ploughings it had taken, by the sun and the air, by rain and by wind; how many harrowings of troubles, disillusionments, wakeful nights; how much living it had needed to sculpt that effigy fit only to be repudiated, that mask of God-alone-knows-who. He touched a hand to his forehead, felt it as naked bone: so stretched was the film of flesh it seemed on the verge of splitting apart. Just a bone, and behind that bone a kind of cement – the doctor's very words – a cement that cramped and strangled the arteries of memory. . .

In God's name let me catch at a memory, he implored – just one! And on the instant, groping, by miracle he found it. A far-off memory, of that selfsame spot and himself as a child, when it was fun to launch fleets of twigs into the water, and follow them along the bank as they raced each other through the eddies, round insidious sandbanks, over rapids. . .

Still today the ground was littered with wisps of straw and splinters of wood. But the ones he chose and threw into the rivulet set off with painful lethargy: no need to lengthen his stride to stay abreast of them. The victory of the humblest of all, a worm-eaten sliver of brushwood, dragged from him the faint acclaim of a grunt, something between a laugh and a cough.

When this subsided his feet instinctively took a turn at playing another childhood game, treading a measure round a smashed guitar high and dry on the stream-bed. Then his voice said "Yes", and he felt an urge to cry.

He did not succumb. No reason to, and he knew it. And yet

something very distressing was happening to him. What it was, perhaps he might understand tomorrow. Or maybe not. Maybe he never would. Just now he felt the need to live the day out like this: nursing his unhappiness, waiting for it to pass, like a child with a pain. And he would leave the bread untouched in his shoulder-bag, he wouldn't sleep, he wouldn't speak to any-one. With the defiant sulks of a child in disgrace. Knights of old, now, didn't they fast on the eve of the battles we read about in story-books? Was it knights or was it saints? Or was it only people about to die? He couldn't say which, his thoughts were flagging, muddling up wishes with memories. It was as if the tiny, transitory interval of the present was crammed with a great crush of yesterdays and tomorrows, a tangle impossible to unravel... Many days had been, others were to come, but he could no longer distinguish past from future, and his fingers, venturing out to touch the mists of existence, met with nothing but air. Fasting purifies the flesh, refines away the ill humours, he had once read somewhere. And yet to him it seemed he was committing an unpardonable transgression, in his eyes every-thing was turned to sin, even his name (he tried calling it aloud) had a harsh, guilty ring to it, like an insincere confession muttered at the grille into God's listening ear.

He glanced over at his gun, leant up against a boundary-stone, its double barrel pointing skywards, very black: the eye-sockets of an evil-hearted blindman. He assessed the lengths... This too had been a game of his, played time and again with the field-guard's old fowling-piece a thousand years ago... He only had to sit on the ground, pop the muzzle in his mouth, and see if his forefinger and thumb hung right, at trigger-level...

It was at this point that he saw the tree, a huge walnut on top of a knoll, charred and solitary. For weeks now fires had been breaking out all over the countryside, set by unknown hands. Hence this tree stood cold and huge on top of a knoll. The trunk, slate-coloured, brought to mind the great walls of lava-blocks he had seen in childhood from the train window, when they took him to Catania to see his father die. Those too had been thus grey and dingy, coming and going in a trice between one tunnel and the next.

He approached it. The walnut was still standing, smoke-blackened, as full of knots and scars as a dying samurai; but the roots were exposed and shrivelled, dangling like entrails into the funnel of soil where the fire had dug deepest. No bud, no sign that this desiccated thing might one day put forth strength; the tree had no more fight left in it than a Capuchin skeleton in its cryptal niche.

The old man stood a moment, then he moved. He knelt and set to digging with his hands, filling his hands with dark clods of earth, firming them in to repair the hollow around the lifeless fibres, performing the gestures of a merciful inhumation.

How rich and dark it was, the soil! How he loved to feel it! The soil nourishes trees, nurses them in its dark like sons. And living creatures too, it succours. It fattens them with worms, it houses them in their season of lethargy. O nourishing rich earth! How right and proper it is that to you we entrust our last remains, our icy, skeletal, ultimate nothing...

He touched his forehead again, and his hands were trembling. So taut was the skin stretched over the bone that very little would it take to strip it bare. In a month, he thought, I shall be bones only, in a year's time nothing but dust...

A scurrying bird brushed against his cheek, was lost among the underbrush, re-emerged from the depths of a blackened crater. It made no move, it scarcely quivered, when he covered it with his hand – a hand as cracked and split as the bark of a tree. He wondered what kind of bird it was – not like any of the birds he knew and went out shooting. He wondered where it came from, where it was going. The old man opened his palm. The bird stayed quite still a moment, then fluttered its wings, flew into a sunbeam, and in a flash was lost to sight.

The sun too vanished now, hid behind a cloud. Then came

a sudden peace, a sudden silence... The old man fell on his knees, embraced the trunk with both arms, pressed his closed lips to one of its furrows, as if by a kiss to impart a leafy hope.

When he picked up his gun and started home, his step was stately as a king's. Where a stone had tumbled from a wall and lay in his path, he bent to recover it, fitted it back in its nook with easy hands. And he sang to himself the while a wordless alleluia.

The Lo Cicero Dossier

FRAGMENT

The report of Dr Fritz Bernasconi

IN SUBMITTING to the attention of this panel of physicians
and students of psychopathy the secret papers of the late
Serafino Lo Cicero, formerly my patient, I cannot deny a certain hesitancy. In the first place on account of their characteristics of fantasizing and extravagance, such as might be expected
from a fabulist by profession and mountebank by nature; and
secondly because the recipient and target of so many outpourings, ramblings and rigmaroles being, in my despite and
unknown to me, none other than myself, I feared from them,
and not without reason, some prejudice to my personal privacy
and professional integrity. So much so that I was more than
once tempted, and you gentlemen will soon understand why,
to expunge a line here and there, where I felt my intentions to
have been most grossly slandered, or when I was blamed for
saying things I never uttered or even thought. Nevertheless, as
is only natural, my mission as a man of science, and my diligence
in the cause of truth, gained the upper hand, my conviction
being that not a whit of this document ought to be removed,
however strongly I doubt that from such a farrago of nonsense,
contrary to what has sometimes been fruitfully achieved on the
basis of the diaries and writings of sufferers from nervous complaints, a diagnosis of any kind is to be obtained. If, in any case,
such a result should be arrived at, I cannot think it will be
by the aid of this evidence alone, but rather with that of the

151

anamnestic and clinical notes recorded during treatment, together with information on a purely human level which faithfully and in the most ample measure I am here to divulge to you, regarding the patient and all his mental vicissitudes during the months (six) of his sojourn at the "Robert Walser" clinic in the Graubunden.

When I first encountered him in my consulting room on September 7 1956, the aforesaid Lo Cicero struck me as a man of robust constitution, although visibly bemused and apparently oppressed in spirit, with ovoidal eyes of which almost nothing was to be seen but the whites, and this in those rare instants when a tic did not cause him to blink and screw them up completely; limping, he informed me, on account of a serious accident he had had in Rome, while negotiating a triple crossroads with his head in the air, in pursuit of a curious cloud; the author of numerous writings in various veins, all unknown to me; a childless widower, now separated after many years of cohabitation from a paintress from the Ciociaria, south of Rome; neurasthenic since childhood; incapable of sleeping more than three hours a night; high blood-pressure; a mysterious, volatile form of diabetes; fits of satyriasis alternating with humiliating bouts of impotence; fifty years old; two or three unmotivated suicide attempts, all the result of an unrestrainable impulse, but always unsuccessful due to glaring ineptitude, if not criminal (*ipse dixit*) carelessness on the part of the aspirant. He came here to Switzerland attracted, he was so good as to say, by my name and reputation, and the fact that I was from the Ticino, he being quite incapable of speaking any other language but Italian. It was his intention, with my help, in some way to become reconciled to himself. With money, now that they were making films of two of his novels, he was well supplied; less so with patience, though he had sufficient to put up with my methods, which he had read about in a newspaper supplement on psychoneurology.

I prescribed the regular analyses and allotted him a single

room on the first floor, overlooking the pinewoods, allowing him from the start, in accordance with his repeated request, to continue to write as much as he liked. As regards reading, without explicitly forbidding it, I advised moderation and unstrenuous choices, perhaps from the classics or at least from authors of a cheerful nature, such as abounded, translated into his language, in the library of the Clinic and on my own personal shelves. From the analyses, with the exception of a former and inactive venereal disorder, which I fear, however, to be the root cause of his troubles, nothing of importance emerged. My sole reason for concern arose from the electrocardiogram, on account of a plummeting T-wave, of which he said with a smile (his smile was utterly charming) that it reproduced the downward curve of his erections. This occasioned some amusement when a few days later, in a further check-up, the wave showed up positive and the graph harmonious, as in a healthy and even sportive heart. I was forced on that occasion to conclude that, though his malady was half of organic origin, for the other half it was certainly spontaneous mental illness, and therefore reasonably open to attack, on condition, on his part, of a resolute alliance with me.

At this point he gave his first exhibition of abnormal behaviour, speaking not a word but simply showing me, palms uppermost, his two hands: damp, pallid, icy-cold, like those of one on the verge of convulsions. When I enquired what on earth he meant by this, he asked me quite out of the blue whether I did not see the stigmata; then, without waiting for an answer, he drew a notebook from his pocket and – whether impromptu or from memory I do not know – he proceeded to scribble verses of an obscene tenor, which I refrain from repeating less from a sense of decency than from the very boredom of them. Student doggerel of very doubtful diagnostic relevance, but available in photocopy (appendix A) at the end of the sheaf of documents distributed a short while ago to each member of the panel. Finally he insisted on returning to his room, demanding a plentiful supply of paper and writing materials. The day following the eccentric behaviour related above his demeanour was already changed. In the space of a few hours he made friends with everyone, stretcher-bearers, medical assistants and nurses. With one of the latter, Gretchen, he assayed certain delicate and tender gallantries, with the effect of leaving the good woman, it seemed to me, somewhat bewildered. To me he offered himself as a well-disposed guinea-pig, wishing, he said, either to recover or to fall ill in earnest, with no more veering back and forth between dead-calm and sea-sickness.

That day saw the beginning of our in-depth study sessions, the details of which I will not report here, all of them being minutely described in appendices B and C. It was during one of these sessions that it occurred to me to suggest that he, being a writer so much given to introversion, should (more for amusement and recreation than anything else) write an action-packed detective story, to see whether it might not in some way canalize his recurrent suicidal urges into innocuous paper-and-ink homicides. He said he would attempt to do so, but that in his case it seemed to him more salutary to give vent to his rancour on some symbolic poppet and personify his grudge as a deceived and disenchanted lover. It was the only reference he made as to his private emotional vicissitudes. During the days I have been speaking of he had given no hint of them whatsoever.

As to the course and results of those sessions, I openly confess that he pulled the wool over my eyes from the very start, passing off as events in his own childhood and youth the experiences of the heroes of tragic dramas and novels, of which I – partly because I had read them so long ago, partly on account of some trusting lenience of mind – did not suspect the counterfeit nature. Until the day my eyes were opened by an all too evident similarity between a mental disorder of his boarding-school days and the adventures of Young Törless. To no avail did I pretend to have long since tumbled to his ruse and to have left him the freedom of his imposture in order to discover eventual identifying mechanisms. He retorted with a sneer that he had selected the texts in no way impelled by the urgings of the unconscious, but in the alphabetical order, from Abélard to Zeno, of a "Companion to European Literature"! From then on I only saw him for random chats, without limitations either as to hours or to subject-matter, though this for the most part centred around two themes, women and death.

In the meanwhile January was upon us, and he, without letting me see a line, wrote on and seemed satisfied with what he wrote. He told me on one occasion that in the course of a few months he was counting on killing as many as three birds with one stone; that is, taking his revenge, effecting his cure and, as the severe Supreme Pontiff of the novel, establishing himself as its Supreme Annihilator. These words caused me some anxiety, for he was indeed showing increasing signs of vainglory, of *folie de grandeur*. He had twice again tried to kill himself, but evidently only to live up to his reputation and by methods even clumsier than usual: poking a finger into an electric point of such low voltage as to be insufficient to stun a fly, and tying a slack string noose to a beam and sticking his head in it a second before Gretchen came to bring him his cup of tea on the dot of five. Childish tricks, at which he was the first to smile. A more serious symptom seemed to me the way he had recently taken to strutting about and casting arrogant glances on all sides, proclaiming himself at every moment to be a superman, a new Lucifer, Socrates and Christ on earth, as well as his continuously carrying on his person the notepad of the book he was writing, clutching it to him even in sleep. His hair, after a while with us, had turned white, with a few yellowish streaks as if the dye had washed out. All day long he would drag his gammy leg, although I once happened to see him in difficulty with the right as opposed to the habitual left, and this disconcerted me. For some time, however, I had ceased to pay particular attention to him. He was by this time refractory to all assistance, but placid enough, more like a lodger than a patient.

He refused therapy of any kind, other than the mildly sedative evening injection. He sometimes gave me the impression of being in better health than I myself, and putting on those fears and that presumptuous air with the sole purpose of making himself out to be ill and being able to indulge himself as such; or even of having fraudulently wormed his way into my establishment intent on making a real-life study of a community of persons disturbed and insane with a view to using them as models for one of his narratives. When he disappeared one morning I confess that I was moved more by curiosity than alarm, although a departure without luggage was not one to be taken lightly. The news, three days later, of his death on a pedestrian crossing in Largo Santa Susanna, knocked down by an ambulance heading at full tilt for the "Gemelli" hospital, could not at that time but strike me as an ironical and more than ambiguous seal set on such a topsy-turvy life, and open to being judged ad lib., as the outcome of a fortuitous accident, or as a conscious and contrived self-sacrifice, or again as a put-up job which unluckily and unhappily turned to tragedy.

It was therefore with uneasiness, agitation and a vague compunction that I decided to look through the manuscript discovered, following his flight, under the bed in the room he had occupied. It is contained in an imitation-leather folder, and before reading it I shall describe its physical characteristics.

The package consists of 117 large sheets, loose but numbered, written by hand with a thick-leaded two-colour correcting pencil. The handwriting is impetuous, almost truculent. Of the colours the blue is vastly prevalent, except for a few words or phrases, more rarely still for entire pages which make sense as a whole and which, in red, every so often break the monologue and are to be understood, in my belief, as fragments of a novel or something of the sort that has been expurgated, if not erased almost entirely; and this with such care as to prevent the text from being restored in any way, leaving these scattered and jumbled minutiae on purpose to intrigue the reader. As for the above-mentioned discourse in blue, though broken and spasmodic it appears to have a coherent thread to it. Addressed, I admit with embarrassment and chagrin, to the present speaker, always in a tone either of wrathful supplication or of bombast and blasphemy, and always with a trace of indelicacy, if not indeed of downright mockery. So much so that I was tempted, as I have already confessed, to expunge a line here and there in defence against slanders on my private life. Or perhaps I should say my honour. Except that on every occasion, I repeat, my duty to science and love of truth gained the upper hand. Concerning which at this point, before I commence the reading, I have a perfect right to speak out and make two matters abundantly clear. They are not alone, but are the two of greatest importance to me. Firstly, that it is not true that I advised Lo Cicero, except in jest and in passing, to write in order to cure himself, since therapies of this sort have no place in my method, nor am I in the habit of promising panaceas to those who in the disturbance of their minds are painfully expiating the erstwhile defects of their forefathers (in this case, hereditary syphilis). Secondly, that my relations with the nurse Gretchen, concerning which malignant statements or insinuations are made in the manuscript, are of transparent professional purity.

Finally, for the better understanding of all present, I state in advance that the narrative fragments in red appear, from certain indications strewn here and there, to be the vestiges of the detective story of which I spoke, albeit humorous and nonsensical, as will be plain to everyone.

I am confirmed in this belief by the list of books requested by Lo Cicero from the hospital library, all of them purely recreational thrillers or works of forensic medicine which subsequently reveal marginal glosses written in ciphers impervious to the most thorough research. A work in a quite different vein, taken out by him and never returned, is Balzac's *Le chef d'oeuvre inconnu*, though I fail to see what use it can have been to him, being in German translation and therefore, to him, entirely unintelligible. . .

Sob-Stuff from a Sleeping-car

SO, LORD GOD...

Here I am in this compartment, "luxury single" they call it, a box five foot by seven and let's say eight foot high. Naked and alone in the night, borne on by blind rails to a city blinder still, whither I am going with the sole aim of leaving again. Naked and alone in the night, stretched on a mattress, arms folded, waiting – I whom no one is waiting for in the world anywhere – waiting... for whom, if not for Thee?

Thee, Thou... The capital letters are Thine by right, enormous absence that art in darkness, existless One existing within me as metaphor of existlessness, invisible One I view in each swift flash of a speeding station, in every glare of acetylene in a tunnel, in each red light or green at points and signals; that I hear in the litany of wheels, *ti-tum ti-tumm, ti-tum ti-tumm*, Honky Tonk Blues on an Odeon 78, and the moon was on the meadows... Lord, I am trotting out words without rhyme or reason, only to keep myself company, to be less alone in my lonesome talk with Thee...

I have set the thermostat needle to my liking. I have put out the three fitted lights: the nightlight behind my head, the large neon strip in the ceiling, the neon tube over the mirror. Hesitant as ever when faced with the battery of push-buttons, fearful of mistakenly pressing the one to call for coffee. I have lowered the blind. I have sealed the door hermetically by rotating the handle: the ticket collector was adamant about this – there are

159

spray-can delinquents abroad at night who give passengers a whiff of gas and rob them in their sleep. Little did he know what a boon sleep would be to me, robbed or otherwise; or how willingly I would exchange this, my dolorous solitude, for a visit from a thief. . .

Here I am then deep in the pitchy night, save only for the unremitting phosphorescence of my wristwatch; safe from all, except from time; hidden from everyone, save for the despotism of Thine eyes, Thy nonchalant clairvoyance.

And now, what now? For how many years have we two duelled unseen by one another. . . like a dog scrapping with the shadow of its own tail. And against each other we wield discrepant weapons, each for that very reason invincible. Thou wieldest the privilege of Thy non-being; I, diversely, that of being, of bodily occupying this hazardous cube of hydrogen and oxygen which stands in the stead of emptiness. A bickering of the deaf to the dumb, words versus silence. Though in truth these of mine are not really words, but a Lamentations, a howl, a shriek lost in the whistling of the train, one with this everlasting Miserere. . .

I thought one time I had caught you red-handed. I heard a shuffling of footsteps, and rasping of breath outside the door of my room. Kneeling down to peek through the keyhole I thought I discerned, on the other side, very close but divided from me by the thickness of the wood, a frozen eyeball. I flung the door open. Needless to say there was no one there.

I don't want to swank, Lord, but I am dying. If I scour the medical dictionary alphabetically, there's not an ailment I have not had or am not anxious to have. And inveterate collector that I am, I yearn to possess them all at once, from Anaemia to Zymotics. I want my body to rebel from top to toe against the fatuous and vain desire that beguiles it into feeling well. I am dying, Lord, and I have tarried all too long, I have been passed over, an alien hand has rigged the shifts and expiry dates. Just when everything seemed ready to round off this square peg for the imminent, mellow, rotund equanimity of death. For, even if few of the many called were to be granted priority, I woefully deluded myself that I could slip through Customs... As was only fair for one tricked into being born flagrantly deficient in understanding and willpower, and lodged *au pair* on earth, albeit strongly averse to the natives and their laws and customs.

Ti-tum ti-tumm, ti-tum ti-tumm... Lord, Thou seest for Thyself, I cannot sleep. My insomnia must have begun in my mother's womb: I skipped the amniotic coma. Clearly I must have been impatient, though heaven knows why! Or else it was caution; for sleeping is such a dangerous thing, a surrender of oneself, bound hand and foot, to a spy, to an unctuous enemy. Every time I succumb to it I live through those scant minutes in secret alarm, repeating to myself, in some niche of the unconscious, that even the most innocent scrap of rapture on my part can be used against me tomorrow, more ineluctably than a thumbprint on the butt of a pistol... Perhaps it is the doctor's fault, for inquisitioning me on waking and making out that all the rivers I wade through in dreams, and the ditches I tumble into, shadow forth my deep-rooted, oft-cited thanatophilia... While I maintain that all of us, from birth, are pregnant with our death, and that it is reasonable, not to say natural, to wish to deliver ourselves of it by dying. Death is a parturition; or, if you prefer, an evacuation. Therefore I never cease to wonder that men do not all of them feel, as I do, from head to foot superfluous on the face of the earth. Even stranger do I find it that this doctor, a man of science, is not aware, instant by instant within himself, of the death of millions of the cells of which he is made; of the ultimate jest ominously edging his fingernails with black; and that he hasn't the nose to scent, in every breath of his and mine, the fetor of an aspirant to corpsehood... Tell

161

him, O Lord, tell him that the Creation is nothing but a stutter
and a blunder. As also is he, and as I am. And as Thou Thyself. . .
Whereas living is such a fire-brand, feverish aberration!

(And as for the suspicion that naught Thou art but a hired
assassin, and that the instigator is Another. . . well this is no
more than the present craze for seeing a hidden hand in
everything.)

Andrea Gothelf, the moribund of sleep, whom I met in a clinic
at Chur during these last years, and with whom every evening
I willingly exchanged much macaronic balderdash about our
common ailment, told me some rather nasty things concerning
Thee, which I don't intend to repeat. He invited me into his
room, I remember, and made himself comfortable. This was
practically a lesson in orthopaedics: glass eye on the bedside
table, false teeth in the glass. . . I was scared he might dismantle
himself to vanishing point. He stopped short of this, but all the
same to some extent he did a bunk, dissolved. Into speech, at
least. About his life gone rotten on him, a fermenting hellbroth,
wine gone sour, undrinkable. He would soon be dead of sleep-
lessness, his was a hopeless case, he was falling to bits. For my
own part, I devoured him with my eyes: death, like every other
exaggeration, never ceases to thrill me. His in particular, which
was a special death, a probable dress-rehearsal for my own.
Wherefore I watched him, I moved among his belongings as in
a simulator for apprentice astronauts, trying to accustom myself
to that air of exquisite catastrophe. . . He showed me his stamp
collection – Luxembourgeoises, Monegasques, Andorrans – all
the rarest issues. I couldn't think of a thing to say, so I whistled
a *Ranz des vaches* in honour of our host nation. But, "My enmity
towards my own body is total," he said quietly. "I can't wait
for that alpenhorn to summon me."

To tell the truth, I couldn't wait for it either. He had the best
room, with wall-to-wall carpeting and view of the Alps, and

(saving everyone else's presence) I wouldn't have minded moving in.

I'm rambling, Lord, but neither of us really has anything to gain by pretending. Thou art no less in question than I am, Thy destiny and health are in my hands. For if it is true that there falls to me only the part of a gabbling puppet, moved by Thy hand and dubbed by the lips, Thy lips, of a ventriloquizing scene-shifter, it is no less true that as soon as Thou art bereft of me Thou also wilt shrink, and fade, and wither to a wraith of smoke, to an intermittent, fugitive echo. Therefore have mercy on me, just as on Thee I have mercy. And keep me company, aloof no longer, within this pirate night I am travers-ing, guided by others, towards a target and a Name. It is what I longed for: that the whirlwind governing me should come to a decision. Though thereupon I ask myself, art Thou then that whirlwind, or art Thou that target? The end and aim of my trajectory or the archer who hits it?

In expectation of this knowledge I persist in scribbling cartels of defiance and tearing them up. It is as a deserter that I wage my campaign of strategic positioning. I falsify the facts, I doctor up the language. I deny myself, but as those women do, who wait beneath the lamplight. I yield myself, yet behind my back I cross my fingers. . .

Lord, let me sleep. Or let me die.

Gretchen, the day before we parted, which was Easter Sunday, taught me the paste-egg game she had played as a child. You wrap up an egg, the most sharp-pointed egg you can find, in the skin of an onion and bind it tightly round and round with a strip of cloth. You hard-boil it and then bury it in an ant-heap, to expose it to the gluey juices secreted by the ants. There it forms an armour plating and is ready to hold its own on impact with any other rival shell of its kind. "This," Gretchen told me,

163

"is what you ought to have done with your heart, before starting to play at life."

She may have been right. Lord, if it be yet seasonable, sheathe this soft yolk and white that is me in an onion skin; and swathe it in a silken kerchief; and set a flame under it; and bury it beside a bush in a nest of friendly ants. . .

Intestatus obiit. . . That will never be said of me. I do nothing but pronounce declarations of intent and perorations for times to come. Never fearing lest the hubbub they raise might shortly trouble the peaceful zero that I will become. These are the dud cheques with which I repay Thy gifts. False coinage versus waste paper – who can tell which of us will in the end have more defrauded the other? Though that's not what counts. . . For after all, I think I have played my part. Opposing every aberration, every monstrous birth, all unreason and treason and loaded dice, every distension and deformation of what is possible. . . opposing them, attempting to oppose them, with the clenched fist of Sufficient Reason and its fourfold knucklebones. But what could I do if every time, Snakes-and-Ladders-like, someone always sent me back to square one? If I felt myself rent asunder, lacerated, and no less vaporous than an angel or a phoenix? If out of all the nibbles and mouthfuls going I never managed to grab a single one? How hard it has been to be me – how much of a mystery. Wonderful even, from time to time, whatever I myself may have thought or said to the contrary. And a hundred times, to be sure, like a bad film or a peevish dream, I would have liked to walk out and leave myself half-way through. To cut clean, cut and run from myself – and goodbye to all that! To fade out of the picture, what could be better? So I need not tell you that this postcard written from crippledom, pen held between my toes, will end with the usual dot dot dot. . .

Life hurts, O Lord. Like a rotten tooth or a trigeminal nerve. And I cast around for swabs, ether, bandages. But the rope grows shorter, narrower the eye of the needle, and up and down in my bedlam puppet-show the figures move no longer. Once upon a time, seated at Thy feet, I was able to play the jester. With bells, and the motley on, and the shoes one red one black...

Be my present help O Lord! Another station or two and we'll be parting...

Lord, Lord...